One Day

NIGHTS SERIES BOOK NINE

A.M. SALINGER

COPYRIGHT

BOOKS BY A.M. SALINGER

NIGHTS

One Night - 1

The Escort - 2

Tokyo Heat - 3

Sweet Obsession - 4

Sweet Possession - 5

The Proposition - 6

Undisclosed - 7

Hush - 8

One Day - 9

Nights Series Short Story Collection

TWILIGHT FALLS

Alex - 1

Carter - 2

Hunter - 3

Wyatt - 4

Drake - 5

Tristan - 6

Miles - 7

Urban Fantasy Romance written as

Ava Marie Salinger

Fallen Messengers

Fractured Souls - 1

Spellbound - 2

Edge Lines - 3

Oathbreaker - 4

Harbinger - 5

Crimson Skies - 6

Wicked - Fallen Messengers Short Story Collection

CHAPTER ONE

Cam Sorvino felt the man beside him stiffen when the flight attendant announced their imminent arrival into Chicago. He reached for Gabe Anderson's left hand where Gabe gripped the armrest of his seat.

"Hey, are you okay?" Cam asked softly, running a finger lightly over Gabe's engagement ring.

Gabe's ice-blue eyes softened as he lowered his gaze to the beautiful, white gold and platinum band adorning his ring finger. "Yes." He turned his hand over and entwined his fingers with Cam's before lifting Cam's hand and pressing a brief kiss to Cam's knuckles. "I'm sorry, I'm just—nervous. I haven't seen them in ten years." He tugged his lower lip between his teeth in a gesture that Cam had come to adore and lowered his head on Cam's shoulder, a heavy sigh shuddering out of him. "I was surprised they agreed to meet me." He paused. "To meet *you*."

Cam frowned faintly over his lover's head as he looked out through the window of the first class cabin to the city growing rapidly below the fuselage of the plane.

It had been his idea for them to reach out to Gabe's parents to invite them to their wedding. Since Cam was an orphan and wouldn't have any family attending on his side, he hadn't wanted Gabe to be in a similar position. He'd first suggested it over breakfast one morning a month ago.

"As long as our friends are there, I don't really mind," Gabe had said. "Besides, my parents pretty much disowned me the day I came out of the closet and told them about—," he'd hesitated for a second and grimaced, "—about Andrew."

Cam had clenched his jaw at the mention of Gabe's former flame. Though he and Gabe were happy and committed to one another, it still irked Cam that Gabe's first gay relationship had ended so disastrously, leaving him with emotional scars that had made it impossible for him to have sex for eight years.

When Gabe confessed to Cam about how Andrew had arranged for a group of five men to gang rape him on camera on the night of their first year anniversary, a night where Gabe had thought he and Andrew would finally consummate their relationship, Cam had wanted to find the bastard and beat the ever-living shit out of him.

That Andrew and his associates had gotten their just deserve and gone on to serve jail sentences didn't take away from the fact that they had hurt and traumatized Gabe so deeply he hadn't been able to bear another man touching him for nearly a decade.

It was thanks to Cam that Gabe had finally been able to defeat his demons and have his first ever gay sexual relation. That he was and always will be Gabe's first man was something Cam treasured with a possessiveness that sometimes scared him.

Although Cam had overcome his trailer trash past and now lived a life he could never have dreamed of when he was a child, Gabe was the first person who had truly belonged to him, in every sense of the word. Yes, they had amazing friends, and that circle had grown to a pretty tight-knit group these past two years, but still, Gabe was his and his alone.

Cam's frown deepened. *And that's something no one will ever take away from me.*

The plane started its descent into Chicago O'Hare Airport. They cleared customs in record time, collected their luggage, and were soon headed for the exit. Cam sensed the tension winding through Gabe increase tenfold when a black limo pulled up smoothly at the curb in front of them as they came out of the building.

He glanced at Gabe's stony expression, surprised. "Hmm. Is that for us?"

Gabe nodded curtly, a muscle jumping in his jawline. The chauffeur got out, greeted them with a polite smile, and ushered them into the back of the vehicle under the curious stares of passers-by.

Cam twisted on the luxurious leather seat and stared at Gabe while the chauffeur placed their cases in the trunk. "Does your family normally do limos?"

Gabe ran a hand through his hair, irritation darkening his face. "I told them we'd get a cab, but my father insisted on sending the car. Knowing him, this is purely for show."

As the vehicle pulled out of the airport and merged onto the interstate heading north, Cam wondered what else he was going to discover about the man he was going to spend the rest of his life with. Gabe had been pretty tight-lipped whenever Cam had inquired after his estranged family in the past. All Cam knew was that Gabe's father worked in banking and his mother used to be a realtor. And he had a younger sister who he'd also lost touch with ten years ago.

The limo rapidly ate away the miles to their destination and soon entered the picturesque North Shore community of Kenilworth, overlooking Lake Michigan. Cam's heart sank as he studied the stunning, multi-million dollar properties visible behind the walls and hedges of the affluent neighborhood they were driving through.

The limo turned into a cul-de-sac, headed through a pair of imposing wrought-iron gates, and pulled into a circular driveway fronting a gorgeous red-bricked Georgian colonial mansion. One of the imposing oak double doors opened to reveal a man in uniform.

"You have a butler?" Cam said leadenly when the vehicle slowed to a smooth stop in front of the solemn figure standing under the portico.

Gabe sighed, turned to face Cam, and took his hands while the chauffeur got out and headed for the trunk. "Okay, before we go in there, I want to apologize."

A bark of laughter escaped Cam. He wasn't sure

whether he was shocked or annoyed with Gabe for having kept this a secret from him. "What, for being stinking rich?"

Gabe shook his head, his expression full of remorse. "My family is wealthy, Cam. I'm not. I'm still the same man you healed that night two years ago. The same man who fell madly in love with you." He leaned his forehead against Cam's. "The same man who belongs to you, body, heart, and soul," he murmured, pressing a sweet kiss to Cam's lips. He pulled back and tightened his hold on Cam's fingers. "No, I'm apologizing for whatever may go down in that house in the next couple of days."

The back door of the limo opened.

"It is good to have you home, Mr. Anderson. Welcome, Mr. Sorvino," the butler murmured respectfully.

Gabe tensed and let go of Cam's hands. Cam followed Gabe's uneasy gaze to the couple watching them coolly from the doorway of the mansion, his lover's heartfelt confession and warning still ringing in his ears.

Oh boy.

CHAPTER TWO

"So, Cameron. Gabe mentioned that you're an asset manager for an investment firm in Asia," Cathy Anderson said in a fake bright voice where she perched on the edge of her Queen Anne chair.

Cam glanced at Gabe where the latter sat stiffly beside him on a Chesterfield sofa.

Although, 'beside' is pushing it slightly. If he were any farther from me, he'd be on the fucking floor.

Cam had noticed how Gabe had maintained a subtle physical distance between them the moment they'd stepped inside his parents' house, as if he were afraid to touch Cam while in their presence. Although this irritated the hell out of Cam, he was willing to follow Gabe's lead on this. For now.

He leveled a steady look at Gabe's mother across the elegant drawing room. "That's right." His lips curved up lopsidedly. "And please, call me Cam."

Gabe's mother blinked under the power of his

smile. Cam's gaze shifted to the man standing behind her.

It was dawning on him that the reason they were here today was because of Gabe's mother. George Anderson's face was still locked in the same chilly expression he'd been wearing since they'd stepped out of the limo half an hour ago. After the initial tepid introductions, Cam was given a grand tour of the mansion and its extensive gardens, complete with swimming pool, tennis courts, and a boathouse sitting on the end of a pier on Lake Michigan.

It was evident to Cam that the senior Andersons were intent on impressing upon him exactly how wealthy they were. He now understood Gabe's comment at the airport about the limo being for show.

"Gabe said you used to be a realtor?" Cam drawled, directing another charming smile at Gabe's mother before he took a sip of his iced tea.

"I was," Cathy said dismissively. "These days, I'm mostly involved in charitable causes."

"That's nice," Cam murmured. "Which ones?"

Surprise darted across Cathy's face at his question. She listed a number of prominent, nonprofit organizations in a puzzled voice.

"Oh. So, nothing allied to the LGBTQ cause?" Cam said in an innocent voice. "You know, lesbian, gay, bisexual, transgender, and *queer*?"

There was a sharp inhale to his right. Cam didn't have to look at Gabe's face to know his lover's eyes had just widened to the size of golf balls.

Cathy's mouth opened and closed silently, her

stunned expression telling Cam she couldn't quite believe he had just said that.

"Umm, no," she finally mumbled, her face pale as she glanced from her son to her husband.

"And George." Cam paused as Gabe's father practically turned to stone behind Gabe's mother. "I'm sorry, may I call you George?"

Icy silence descended around them.

"You may," George Anderson finally bit out.

"Gabe told me you're a banker," Cam said blithely.

George frowned. "I was," he said with a grunt.

Gabe straightened at the other end of the couch. "You retired?" he asked, stunned.

George's mouth thinned into a hostile line as he looked at his son.

"Yes," Cathy replied awkwardly in his stead. "Your father had a heart attack a couple of years ago. The doctors ordered him to take early retirement."

Gabe blinked owlishly at his parents. "You had a heart attack?" he asked his father hoarsely.

This time, Cam literally felt Gabe's shock. Unheeding of Gabe's parents, he moved along the couch and took Gabe's left hand where the latter clutched his thigh in a white-knuckled grip, his heart aching for the man he loved.

"And you never—" Gabe stopped and swallowed convulsively, his voice echoing with grief. "You never called to tell me?!"

Something that looked like guilt darted in Cathy's eyes. George's gaze dropped to where Cam held Gabe's hand, the muscle jumping in his cheek and the scowl darkening his features telling Cam everything he needed to know with regards to how the man viewed his and Gabe's relationship and engagement.

Cam was about to throw caution to the wind and tell Gabe's parents exactly what he thought of them when a knock came at the drawing room door. It opened to reveal a woman dressed in a conservative business suit that made her look much older than her age.

"I'm sorry I'm late," she said breathlessly as she strode past the butler. "I got delayed at the office—" She stopped in her tracks when she saw Cam and Gabe. "Oh." Blue eyes identical to Gabe's widened slightly as she took in their linked hands and George Anderson's disapproving expression.

GABE ROLLED ONTO HIS SIDE, PLUMPED UP THE PILLOW under his head, and lay back down again. He sighed for what felt like the umpteenth time that day.

What a fucking disaster.

He'd known from the word go that this was a bad idea when Cam first suggested it a month ago. Although he was aware Cam only had his best interests at heart, Gabe had tried numerous times to convince his fiancé that they didn't need to invite the Andersons to the wedding. Or go see them when he'd gotten the surprise letter from his mother requesting Gabe and Cam come visit so they could meet with them.

Cam being Cam, he'd had none of it.

And now, here we are, sleeping in different rooms because my parents can't even bear the thought of us being physically together under their roof.

Gabe grimaced as he recalled Cam's face an hour ago, when the butler had shown them to the guest quarters after dinner.

"This is your room, Mr. Sorvino," the man said, indicating a door. He hesitated and looked at Gabe. "Mr. Anderson, your old room awaits you in the family wing."

Cam froze. "I'm sorry, what?"

The butler paled slightly under Cam's steely stare. "Mr. and Mrs. Anderson, er, insisted on separate sleeping arrangements."

"Separate sleeping arrangements?" Cam repeated incredulously. He gave Gabe a "Are-you-fucking-kidding-me-right-now?" look over the butler's shoulder. "For their son and his fiancé?"

The butler swallowed and dipped his chin stiffly, an apologetic expression washing across his face.

"It's alright, Cam," Gabe murmured. "It's only for two nights."

"It's two more nights than I can tolerate, Gabe!" Cam hissed. "And I can't believe you're actually thinking of going along with this. This is not the fucking eighteenth century!"

Gabe straightened, anger flickering through him in that moment. "Cam, let it go," he said in a hard voice. "We knew what we were getting ourselves into when we came here. We have to abide by their wishes."

Cam stared at him for a moment, a muscle working in his jawline. "Shit." He stormed inside the guest bedroom and slammed the door shut.

"I'm sorry, Mr. Anderson," the butler mumbled to Gabe.

"It's okay," Gabe said, his stomach twisting as he gazed at the closed door. *"It's not your fault."*

Gabe resigned himself to what was likely going to be a sleepless night, turned on his back, and stared at the dark ceiling. Sorrow filled him as he thought of the stilted conversations and the strained dinner he and Cam had shared with his parents and his sister Melissa since they'd arrived at what used to be his home.

Gabe couldn't really fault his upbringing. Although his father was a strict man who never cared to show his feelings, Gabe knew he'd loved him deep down inside. As had his mother and his sister, despite their own increasingly reserved attitudes while he was growing up, his father's rigid expectations squashing much of the warmth and spontaneity they used to display when he was a child.

All that changed when he came home for his final spring break from college and confessed to them what he'd suspected for a number of years; that he was gay.

It had taken all of Gabe's courage to stand in his own drawing room that day and tell his parents and his sister that not only did he like men, he was in his first ever relationship with one.

He had been prepared for their shock and anger. He had even been prepared for the fact that they might stop talking to him for some time. What he hadn't expected was that they would cut him off from their lives completely, with a cool, clinical precision worthy of a surgeon's blade.

An age-old agony pierced through Gabe then, so sharp it almost winded him.

What he hadn't told Cam was that he came out to his family and was rejected by them ten days before Andrew arranged for him to get gang raped on camera. When he'd been taken to the ER by the cops that night and asked for his next of kin's details, Gabe had literally frozen. For one wild moment, he'd been tempted to give the detective and the nurse his parents' address and phone number. Then he'd recalled his mother and his sister's shocked faces and the revulsion in his father's eyes.

Now that he'd seen how little his family's attitude had changed in the last ten years, Gabe was glad he hadn't done so at the time. The thought of how much worse they could have made things, or even more devastatingly, chosen not to turn up, was something that had gnawed at him all evening.

Gabe relaxed his stiff shoulders and was urging himself to go to sleep when his cell dinged on the night stand. He reached for the phone, read the message on the screen, and smiled faintly as some of his tension eased.

Cam: I'm sorry for being an asshole.

CHAPTER THREE

CAM BREATHED A SIGH OF RELIEF WHEN GABE REPLIED TO his text.

> Gabe: You were. One giant asshole.

Cam glanced around the luxurious guest room in the soft glow of the nightstand lamp from where he sat on the bed, his back propped on a pillow against the headboard. He tapped out another message.

> Cam: This room is nice and all, but I'd rather be in your bed right now.

Gabe replied immediately.

> Gabe: Well, you can't. House rules.

Cam pursed his lips.

> Cam: The house rules suck.

> Gabe: Not that I want to gloat or anything, but I told you so.

Cam frowned at that. An evil smile curved his lips in the next instant. He keyed in a reply.

> Cam: Did I ever tell you how much I like breaking rules?

He chuckled when his cell rang two seconds later.

"You had better not come over here, Cameron Sorvino!" Gabe hissed in his ear. "I will never hear the end of it if my parents hear us having sex!"

Heat flashed through Cam. Although he knew Gabe couldn't see him, he arched an eyebrow. "Who said anything about having sex?"

Awkward silence descended on the line. Gabe cursed under his breath.

Cam's cock stirred. *I bet he's blushing right now.*

A devilish idea came to him in that instant.

"Is that what you thought we'd be doing, Gabe?" Cam said, deliberately dropping his voice to the husky octave that made Gabe go wild in bed.

The sound of Gabe's breath shuddering out of him was all it took for Cam's dick to come to full attention. He dropped a hand to his groin and imagined Gabe doing the same where he lay in his own bed on the other side of the mansion.

"Do you want that, Gabe?" Cam continued throatily as he started stroking himself through his pajamas. "Do you want me to come over there, climb on top of you, spread your thighs with my hands, and stick my thick cock inside your hole?"

Gabe's sultry hum echoed softly in Cam's ears. "Hmm. You can't."

"Then how about you show me instead?" Cam said, slipping a hand inside his pajamas to palm his naked dick.

"*What?!*" Gabe squealed after a shocked pause.

"You heard me right the first time, you little tease," Cam said, a hiss of pleasure slipping out of him as he stroked a thumb across the sensitive head of his cock. "Now, turn your phone camera on and show me what I'm gonna be missing for the next two nights."

For a moment, Cam thought Gabe would refuse.

"Can you see?" Gabe finally said in that breathless voice that told Cam he was turned on as fuck.

Cam's pulse spiked. He snatched the cell from his ear, his hand stilling on his swollen dick while he stared intently at the screen. He could barely make out Gabe's shadowy shape against the gloomy background.

"Switch your bedside lamp on," Cam said. He sat up straighter against the headboard and kicked the bedcovers off his legs while Gabe twisted and flicked a switch.

Gabe's mussed up hair and flushed face came into view in the golden light. He was wearing a gray T-shirt and matching checkered pajama bottoms.

"Strip," Cam said, excitement sending his heart thundering against his ribs.

Gabe blinked, shock flaring across his face. "I—" He

stopped and glanced at something at the opposite end of the room.

The door, probably.

"Do the house rules say you can't get naked under your own roof?" Cam said.

Gabe hesitated before biting his lip and shaking his head.

"Then strip, Gabe," Cam ordered silkily.

Color bloomed on Gabe's cheeks at Cam's command. Cam knew how much Gabe loved it when he took that tone in the bedroom and dominated him during sex.

A view of Gabe's bedroom ceiling appeared for precious seconds while he put the phone down and got off the bed, the rustle of clothes telling Cam he was undressing.

Gabe's naked ass flashed past the cell camera as he climbed back on the mattress. He picked up the phone and gazed at Cam heatedly.

Cam groaned at the sight of Gabe's bare chest and nipples. "More." He yanked his own pajamas down his hips and freed his aching cock. "I want to see all of you."

The way Gabe's eyes darkened and he tugged his lower lip sexily between his strong, white teeth told Cam how much that idea was blowing his mind.

The camera view changed jerkily while Gabe grabbed a pillow and propped the cell against it at the end of the bed. Cam's mouth went dry as he watched Gabe place another pillow against the headboard and settle there.

"Fuck, that's hot," Cam whispered, his hand getting busy on his dick once more while his greedy eyes roamed Gabe's delicious, naked body.

Gabe's chest rose and fell with his heavy breaths where he sat on his bed. His blue eyes were dark with passion and his swollen cock was already leaking pre-cum.

"Touch yourself, Gabe," Cam said, tingles of pleasure dancing through his rock-hard shaft as he rubbed himself. "Show me what you want me to do to you."

Gabe hesitated before dropping his right hand to his cock. He closed his fingers around the base of his shaft and stroked them up in a slow, wicked move that made Cam curse.

"Jesus, Gabe!" Cam growled, his hand clenching painfully on his own cock to stop himself from coming there and then. "I want to walk out of this room, come over there, and suck your dick until you're bone dry!"

"Cam!" Gabe moaned, hips rolling and jerking off the mattress as he set himself a sweetly punishing pace, his fingers slick with pre-cum where he worked his glistening flesh.

"Show me, Gabe," Cam ordered between clenched teeth. "Show me *everything* you want me to do to you."

Gabe's hand stilled on himself for a moment. His gaze grew hooded as he stared straight at the camera. Then, he brought his left hand to his lips.

Blood roared in Cam's ears as he watched Gabe suck two fingers into the hot depths of his mouth and make them nice and wet all the way to the second knuckles.

Holy shit.

Cam's breathing froze when Gabe took his fingers out with a wet popping sound and brought them down to his groin. He widened his legs and slipped his slick digits in the crease beneath his twitching balls.

"More," Cam whispered hoarsely. "Your legs. Spread them more."

Gabe panted and obeyed, bending his knees and spreading his thighs wide open. He tilted his hips forward until his pink pucker was finally exposed to the camera.

"Fuck!" Cam hissed at the wicked sight of Gabe touching and rubbing his own ass.

As if he knew exactly what Cam wanted to see next, Gabe slipped one, then two fingers past the tight rings of muscles guarding his entrance. A hum of pleasure vibrated out of him and he arched his back beautifully against the headboard while he seated his digits fully inside himself.

Cam gritted his teeth. "Does it feel good, Gabe?"

Gabe blinked dazedly at the camera.

Cam cursed again as Gabe tightened himself around his fingers, his hole clenching and contracting lewdly, sucking his two digits in even more.

"*Yessss!*" Gabe whimpered. "It's good." He tugged his lower lip between his teeth as he withdrew his fingers and thrust them back inside his hole, a guttural sound leaving him. "But not as good as your dick, Cam." He repeated the move and continued working his rock-hard shaft, fucking his ass with one hand while he rubbed himself sensuously with the other.

Sweat beaded Cam's upper lip as he watched the decadent show Gabe was putting on for him. He accelerated the pace of his hand on his own throbbing cock.

Gabe writhed and danced in front of the camera, his right hand occasionally leaving his leaking cock to tug and twist at his hard nipples while he carried on thrusting his fingers in and out of his spasming ass.

Tension wound through Cam as the first pulse of his orgasm danced down his spine. "*Oh fuck, Gabe!* I'm getting close!"

"Yes!" Gabe sang, his hands moving faster and faster on and inside himself as he rolled his hips, his sweat-slick chest glistening in the soft light bathing his room.

"Shit!" Cam groaned. "Find something to bite down on!"

Gabe stared fuzzily at the camera.

"You know how loud you get when you come!" Cam panted, pushing down on the explosive climax coiling in the pit of his belly and his balls.

Gabe leaned sideways and grabbed his T-shirt from the floor. He shoved a mouthful of it between his teeth, grabbed his dick, and slid down the bed slightly. He widened his thighs even more, worked his hole with powerful thrusts of his fingers, and stroked and rubbed his shaft and the head of his cock, his keens and moans muffled by the material.

"*Fuck, fuck, fuck!*" Cam chanted between clenched teeth as his climax finally hit him. He thrust his hips jerkily off the bed while his cock exploded and spurted thick streams of cum all over his belly, pleasure sending blood thundering in his ears and causing his vision to flicker with white light.

Gabe stilled on the screen. He bowed his spine and came violently, his corded neck and face flushed a dull crimson as he stifled his cries of pleasure, ass dancing off the mattress and dick trembling and jerking while it shot sticky white jets all up his chest.

So beautiful. God, he's so fucking beautiful!

Cam's heart pounded savagely in his chest as he stared at Gabe, his own body slowly relaxing in a warm, post-orgasmic glow as the final pulses of his climax started to fade.

Gabe joined him there a moment later, his blue eyes opening languorously where he'd sagged against the headboard, red flags of color still painted across his cheekbones. He removed the damp T-shirt from his mouth and dropped it onto the floor, his pants loud across the connection as he slowly straightened his legs.

"Hmm," Cam purred. "I want to come over there and lick that sweet stuff off your body."

Gabe groaned, a muffled chuckle escaping his swollen lips where he'd bitten and gnawed them during his explosive orgasm. "Don't you dare, you beast."

"Can we do this again tomorrow night?" Cam said.

Gabe blinked on the screen. "You're joking, right?"

"Does this look like my joking face?" Cam said testily. He grabbed his cock and angled his phone so the camera was pointed at his groin.

"No, that looks like your well-used dick," Gabe said breathlessly. "Fuck, I want that inside me."

Cam grinned and tilted the camera so he was looking at Gabe again. "So, that's a yes to more phone sex?"

Gabe rolled his eyes. "Yes, you ass."

CHAPTER FOUR

They were having breakfast in the greenhouse the next morning when Gabe's father dropped a bombshell.

"After further discussion, we've decided that it would not be convenient for us to attend your wedding," George said calmly where he sat drinking coffee at the head of the table. "You are welcome to continue visiting with us until you leave tomorrow."

Gabe's stomach dropped. His mother's fingers stilled on her knife and fork where she was cutting into her poached egg opposite him. A faint frown danced across his sister's face where she sat beside her.

Gabe carefully put his own cutlery down and turned to look at his father, the little appetite he'd had since they'd sat down at the breakfast table gone. Anger surged through him as he studied the man watching him with a cold expression. He'd thought that when the invitation was extended for him and Cam to come here, it meant his family had finally come to terms, however grudgingly, with his sexuality and that they had unofficially agreed to attend his and Cam's wedding. He was about to ask his father exactly what the inconvenience was when Cam spoke beside him, stealing the words from his mouth.

"And what, pray tell, do you mean by that?" Cam said in a silky voice that told Gabe he was seconds away from blowing his fuse.

Gabe reached under the table and grasped Cam's hand where he'd fisted it on his knee.

George's gaze switched from Cam to Gabe. He arched an eyebrow. "You can't honestly expect us to forgive and forget what you did, Gabe. What you are, in fact, still doing."

Gabe felt the blood drain from his face at the blatant condemnation in his father's eyes.

"George," Cathy whispered pleadingly, her expression ashen as she stared at her husband.

A vein throbbed in Melissa's temple. She put her cup of coffee down with a thunk that drew everyone's gaze.

George frowned. "Do you have something to say, Melissa?"

"It doesn't matter whether I have something to say or nor, does it, Dad?" Melissa said between clenched teeth.

Gabe blinked, surprised at the animosity he could read in Melissa's eyes as she glared at their father. Then Cam was rising to his feet beside him.

"Why exactly did you ask us to come and meet with

you if you'd already made up your mind?" Cam said icily. "Was it to humiliate us?" He glanced at Gabe. "To humiliate *him?*"

"Cam," Gabe murmured. He got up and touched Cam's shoulder, shocked at the rage vibrating through his lover. "Please, don't make a—"

"What, make a scene?" Cam interrupted. He looked from Gabe's stricken expression to the man at the head of the table. "The one making the scene here is your father, Gabe." He cast his napkin on the table, clasped Gabe's hand tightly, and glared at Gabe's father. "I pity you." He glanced at Cathy and Melissa. "I pity all of you. Because you don't see it. You don't see how beautiful Gabe is inside and out."

Gabe's breath caught at the love and adoration blazing out of Cam's stormy gray eyes.

"I was a broken man when I met your son," Cam said to George and Cathy. "I was someone who wasn't capable of love. Someone who'd spent his entire adult life determined never to get hurt again, like his own mother had hurt him when he was a child. All that changed the day I met Gabe." He turned, cradled Gabe's face lightly with his free hand, and pressed a gentle kiss to his forehead. "He taught me so much. How to love. How to laugh. How to fight and make up. And every day that I spend with Gabe is another day I thank God for the gift He granted me when He gave me your son."

Tears blurred Gabe's vision. He heard a sniff from across the way and wasn't sure if it'd come from his mother or his sister. He wiped his eyes with the back of his hand, unable to tear his gaze from the face of the man he loved.

"So, yes, I pity you," Cam said. A scowl darkened his features. "That you're still unable to accept Gabe for who he is, even after everything he went through ten years ago at the hands of Andrew is something I can't—"

Gabe closed his eyes at the same time his mother gasped out, "What do you mean? What did—what did Andrew do?!"

Cam's fingers clenched around Gabe's.

Gabe took a deep breath and opened his eyes to meet Cam's shocked stare, his legs so weak he thought he might fall but for Cam's steady grip.

"They don't know?" Cam asked him harshly.

"Don't know what?" Melissa said on the other side of the table, her knuckles white on her napkin.

Gabe swallowed convulsively as he gazed at Cam. "I —I never told them. I—," his voice broke slightly, "—I couldn't. It happened ten days after I came out to them."

Cam swore, let go of Gabe's hand, and closed his arms around Gabe in a fierce embrace. "*God, Gabe!* You mean you went through that hell by yourself?!" His voice trembled as he buried his face in Gabe's hair.

"If something happened between Gabe and his— *boyfriend*," George spat out, "he has no one to blame but himself for his lifestyle choices."

Gabe froze in Cam's arms. He shut his eyes tightly once more, shame and anger swirling through him in equal measure at his father's cruel words, the memories from that horrific night washing over him in giant waves that threatened to drown him.

It was only the warmth and solid strength of the man who was holding him in that moment that saved him from falling completely into the abyss.

"*George!*" Cathy snapped.

"Dad! That's a horrible—" Melissa started.

&

"So, YOU THINK YOUR SON DESERVED TO BE DRUGGED BY someone he trusted and gang raped on camera?" Cam said in a low voice, the rage burning through him so strong he feared he'd bite his tongue off.

A shocked cry escaped Cathy. Melissa rose to her feet and clutched her mother's shoulder.

"You truly believe that Gabe warranted that terrible fate because he's *gay?*" Cam roared, his gaze on the man at the head of the table.

George Anderson had turned to stone where he sat.

"That he deserved to be so emotionally scarred by that experience he couldn't let another person touch him for eight years and had to move to another country to start afresh, even after hundreds of hours of therapy?!" Cam growled while Gabe shivered and trembled in his arms. "Well, if that's what you truly think, then we have nothing else to say to one another!"

Cam stepped back and cradled Gabe's face gently in his hands. His heart throbbed at the hurt and guilt in the beautiful blue eyes opposite his. "I'm leaving. Are you coming with me?"

Gabe shuddered. He inhaled shakily and nodded once, fingers rising to clutch Cam's wrists, clinging to him as if he were his lifeline. Cam kissed the tear drops on Gabe's eyelashes, took his hand, and led him out of greenhouse.

Cathy and Melissa were standing in the foyer when they came down minutes later with their suitcases.

"Gabe," Cathy said tremulously, her eyes red and her face ghostly pale. "Please, don't go. We can talk this—"

Cam took the wedding invitation out of his jacket and pressed the envelope in her hand. "I doubt we'll see you there." He glanced at Melissa's stricken expression. "But that's where it's happening, just in case."

"I'm sorry," Gabe whispered. He walked over to his mother and sister and hugged them gently. "I can't—I just can't—" He turned and headed out of the front door of his home, Cam following in his steps.

CHAPTER FIVE

"Will you forgive me?" Cam said forlornly.

Gabe sighed, reached across the table, and stabbed one of Cam's scallops with a fork.

"Can you stop apologizing already and enjoy the food and the view?" he muttered before biting down on the succulent meat. He picked up his glass of wine and indicated the spectacular night time vista of the city spread out beyond the window next to them.

They were in one of the most exclusive restaurants in downtown Chicago. It had been two days since Gabe had left his parents' house after the explosive confrontation with his father. He and Cam had checked in early to the hotel where they had intended to stay for a week before traveling back to Tokyo and had spent the last forty-eight hours in a whirlwind of sight-seeing and shopping. Although Gabe's mother and sister had tried to contact him in the past couple of days, Gabe hadn't taken their calls or responded to their messages, too bruised still from the incident with his father.

Cam pursed his lips. "But it's because of me that you got hurt again."

Gabe cursed under his breath. "Look, Cam. It's not your fault my father has a giant stick up his ass, and my mother and sister won't stand up to him to tell him to take the damn thing out."

Cam blinked. "I'm sorry," he blurted, "but that image is just wrong. In so many ways."

Gabe stared at him before bursting out laughing.

Cam smiled, his shoulders relaxing for the first time that day. "So, you forgive me?"

"There's nothing to forgive," Gabe said. "At least now we know where we stand with them."

Cam studied him thoughtfully. "You never know. People can change. I did."

Gabe's heart swelled at the warmth in Cam's gaze. His cell buzzed in his pocket. He frowned and took it out, half expecting to see another message from his mother or sister. His brow cleared when he saw the text.

"Oh-oh," Gabe said with a chuckle. "I'm afraid I'm gonna have to make myself scarce for a moment. It's Operation Secret Squirrel."

Cam groaned. "What the heck does he want now?"

"Don't know," Gabe said. He put his napkin down and rose from the table. "But, since the guy *is* one of our best men and in charge of organizing our combined bachelor party, I best reply before he gets cranky."

Cam scowled. "Tell him I still think Operation Secret Squirrel is a stupid code name."

"Yeah, yeah," Gabe murmured, dropping a kiss on Cam's cheek. He turned and headed for a quiet section of the bar before hitting dial.

Ethan Skye answered on the first ring. "Wow. I'm surprised you called me so fast. I thought Cam would have you pinned under him somewhere and doing the dance of the two-headed beast."

Gabe sighed at his best friend's usual filthy banter. "Cam and I do have lives and jobs, you know. We don't just spend all our time fucking."

Ethan sniffed. "That's a shame. I spend a lot of my time doing just that with Joe."

"That's because you live and work together," Gabe drawled. "Akihito threatened to start a 'sex jar' for you to pay into for the number of times you drag Joe up to the apartment above the club in the middle of a shift. He said he'd be able to retire within five years if he did."

"We only ever do it when I'm on break," Ethan said defensively. "Plus, it keeps us fit."

"Sure it does," Gabe said with a grin. "Anyway, what's up? Do you need something from us for the bachelor party?"

There was a pause at the end of the line

"No," Ethan said quietly. "There's something I've been meaning to talk to you about. Something that's been on my mind a lot lately. I'm hoping you'll come on board with me on this particular project. If you agree, then there's something I need you to do before you leave the States."

Gabe frowned at Ethan's serious tone. His eyes widened when Ethan started explaining what it was exactly he was doing and why he wanted Gabe in on it. By the time Ethan finished talking, Gabe's palms were sweaty and his heart was racing in his chest.

"Yes," he breathed. "Count me in."

"You sure?" Ethan said hesitantly.

Gabe glanced across the restaurant to where Cam sat digging into his steak. "Absolutely."

"Okay," Ethan said, relieved. "I'll send you the details and you can arrange to meet him at your convenience. You think you'll manage to ditch Cam for a couple of hours?"

Gabe smiled, excitement coursing through him at what Ethan had proposed. "I'll come up with something. And Ethan?"

"Yeah?"

"Thank you," Gabe said, closing his eyes briefly. "If this works, it will change all of our lives. For the better, I hope."

"I know," Ethan said. He paused. "To be honest, it scares the ever living shit out of me. There's a good chance it'll fail and he'll come up with nothing. But, there's also a chance he might."

"Yes." Gabe thought of his family and the hell that had been the last few days. "We could really do with some luck right now."

"The meeting with your parents went as badly as you thought it would?" Ethan said sympathetically.

"It was worse," Gabe admitted.

"Shit," Ethan murmured. "I'm sorry."

"It's alright," Gabe said. "Having Cam with me helped a lot."

"I want to know all the details but I gotta go," Ethan said. "Joe's coming out of the shower."

"I'll text you later," Gabe said. He ended the call and took a moment to compose himself before returning to his and Cam's table, his mind buzzing from the conversation he and Ethan had just shared.

"Everything okay?" Cam said curiously as Gabe took his seat.

"Uh-huh," Gabe said, flashing him a smile.

"What did Ethan want?" Cam muttered.

Gabe placed his elbows on the table and fixed Cam with a solemn stare. "He wanted to know your exact length and girth. He's thinking about having a dick cake made. Scaled up, obviously."

Cam slowly lowered his meat-laden fork to his plate, his gray eyes widening with horror. "I swear to God, I will fucking *kill* Ethan if he—" He stopped and scowled when Gabe snorted and burst out laughing. "You ass."

"I'm sorry!" Gabe managed between chuckles. "You should have seen the expression on your face."

Cam narrowed his eyes at him before catching the attention of a passing waitress. "Excuse me, could I have a plate of fresh oysters?"

Gabe gave him a puzzled look. "What are the oysters for? We've already ordered."

Cam flashed him an evil smile. "It's for your punishment tonight."

Gabe shivered at the flash of heat in Cam's eyes. *Shit.* "He doesn't need oysters," he said hastily to the waitress. "Trust me on this."

The woman's face reddened as she glanced between them.

Cam arched an eyebrow at Gabe. "Who said the oysters were for me?"

Gabe groaned. *Oh God.*

The last time Cam had made him have oysters, he'd spent the night horny as hell and had been teased to within an inch of life during the long hours of sex play Cam had indulged in with his over-sensitive body.

Gabe gnawed his lower lip in anxious anticipation after the waitress left their table. "How bad is this going to be?"

Cam reached across the table and pressed a thumb to Gabe's lip, stopping him from chewing it. "As bad as you want it to be," he said in a gravelly voice that sent another shiver down Gabe's spine. "Or rather, as good."

Gabe's heart stuttered at the fiery passion burning brightly in Cam's eyes.

I will never tire of this man. Whatever he wants. Whenever he wants it. I will accept it all. All of him. Forever.

CHAPTER SIX

Ethan startled and blinked at Eveline. "Nothing. Why?"

Eveline gave him a faintly bemused smile across the restaurant table where they sat having lunch. "You seem a bit distracted."

"Oh. Sorry, I was just thinking about Gabe and Cam's bachelor party," Ethan said in a light voice he hoped masked his lie.

Eveline narrowed her eyes at him. "Speaking of which, I see the need to keep the location and details a secret from the grooms, but how come the rest of the guests are being kept in the dark too?"

Ethan grinned. There were ten of them joining Gabe and Cam on their bachelors' gig in three weeks. He and his lover Joe Cavendish, Eveline Claude and Lincoln Hudson, Rhys Damon and Wade Tucker, Ash Colby and Luke Rutherford, and Lana Keele and Tom Sutherland. Only Ethan knew the juicy particulars of the where and what of the weekend-long party. And if he was right, the grooms and their guests were going to positively love what he'd planned for them.

"It's a surprise," he said, flashing a saucy wink at Eveline.

She sighed. "So what, we're just supposed to turn up at the airport? You're not even gonna give us a hint as to what we should pack?"

"Swim suit, formal evening wear, and some casual day clothes," Ethan said promptly.

Eveline raised her eyebrows. "Swim suit?"

"Yup," Ethan said. "I've sent Luke's flight crew instructions to give to Luke and Ash. And Tom and Lana since he'll be picking them up from Shanghai on the way."

Eveline rolled her eyes at him and stabbed a spring roll with her chopsticks. They finished lunch and were headed out of the restaurant door with their shopping bags when Ethan's cell buzzed in his jeans. He slipped the phone out of his rear pocket and tensed when he saw the number on the screen.

"Sorry, Evie. I gotta take this," he mumbled.

Eveline nodded at him as they walked out into the bright, Sunday afternoon sun. Ethan slowed his pace, pressed the answer button, and brought the cell to his ear.

"Hey, Gabe," he said in a low voice as he strolled up the quiet cul-de-sac where the restaurant was located, Eveline a few steps ahead of him.

"We're at the airport, headed back to Tokyo," Gabe

started without preamble. "I thought you'd want to know. I met him last night."

Butterflies swarmed Ethan's stomach. "And?"

"He's already got a couple of leads to work on," Gabe said, his tone full of excitement. "He's going to keep digging into the records he's found." Gabe hesitated. "He warned me not to get our hopes up though."

Ethan closed his eyes briefly, his heart twisting with a mixture of happiness and apprehension at his best friend's words. "I know. But I can't stop myself from wishing this will actually lead somewhere."

"So do I," Gabe said wholeheartedly. "He'll be giving us a weekly update from now on."

"Great," Ethan said. The sound of an engine drew his attention. He looked up and saw a black SUV turn the corner and start down the road toward them. "Thanks for doing this, Gabe. Let's catch up when you—"

The SUV screeched to a halt next to Eveline. She stopped and looked at the vehicle curiously. Two men got out of the front and headed purposefully toward her.

Hairs rose on the back of Ethan's neck. "Gabe, I gotta go," he said hastily into his cell. "Call me when you get back." He ended the call and pocketed the phone.

"Miss Claude?" one of the men asked in a clipped voice as Ethan joined Eveline.

"Yes?" she said in a puzzled tone.

Ethan positioned himself slightly in front of

Eveline. His eyes narrowed as he got his first good look at the two men. They were big and built like tanks, their suits and stance screaming some kind of security detail.

Something told Ethan they were trouble.

The men scrutinized him from behind their black sunglasses for a couple of beats.

"Senator Hudson would like a word with you, Miss Claude," the first man said to Eveline coolly over Ethan's shoulder. "Please come with us."

Eveline stiffened behind Ethan. "What?"

Ethan frowned. Senator Harry Hudson was Lincoln's estranged father. As far as he knew from what Eveline had revealed to him, the two men hadn't been on speaking terms for over a decade. Their relationship had soured even further as of late, after the senator discovered his one and only son was going out with a former escort.

"What do you mean Senator Hudson wants to have a word with me?" Eveline said in a hardening voice. Ethan saw her glance at the SUV out of the corner of his left eye.

The first man stepped to the side and reached around Ethan.

Ethan twisted and grabbed the stranger's wrist before his fingers made contact with Eveline's arm. "Whoa! Let's not get ahead of ourselves, shall we? The lady hasn't agreed to anything."

A hand landed heavily on Ethan's right shoulder.

"Step aside, kid," the second man said with a heavy frown, his fingers clenching warningly into the material of Ethan's T-shirt. "This has nothing to do with you."

Ethan looked between the two men before glancing up the road. He gritted his teeth. There was no one else in sight.

Fuck. I'm not sure if I can take both of them on.

"Now, if you could just get into the back of the vehicle," the first man said to Eveline.

Eveline's eyes widened. She stared at the blackout windows of the SUV. "What's this about? Is he—is Lincoln's father *in there?!*"

"No," the man replied. "But he wants to talk to you. From a more private location."

Ethan swore when the guy gripping his shoulder suddenly grabbed his arms and wrenched them behind his back. His bags thudded to the ground as he stumbled backward on the narrow sidewalk.

"Hey! What the hell are you—," Eveline started, stepping toward them.

The first man took hold of Eveline's arm and halted her stride. She froze, her gaze slowly dropping to where he gripped her flesh.

Fear sent Ethan's pulse rocketing toward the stratosphere. He cursed and started to struggle in his assailant's grip. "You asshole!" he hissed at the man clutching Eveline's arm. "Let go of her—"

Eveline scowled.

CHAPTER SEVEN

"SHE DID *WHAT*?!" LINCOLN ROARED DOWN THE PHONE line.

Ethan winced as he held an improvised ice compress to his bloodied lower lip.

"Evie beat the shit out of the guys your father hired to intimidate her," he mumbled into his cell. "She was like a fucking ninja, Linc," he added, not bothering to hide the admiration in his voice. He glanced across the police station's reception to the glass window of the interrogation room where Eveline sat giving her deposition to a female detective. A muscle ticked in Eveline's cheek while she spoke to the woman. Her arms were crossed across her chest and her left knee bounced impatiently under the table. "By the looks of it, she's still pissed. You'd better get here."

"Give me twenty minutes!" Lincoln barked. "No. Fifteen!"

Ethan realized he was listening to the dial tone. He sighed and tucked his phone into his rear pocket. The front doors of the police station banged open to his right, startling him.

Joe Cavendish stormed inside the reception, ignored the sergeant staring at him from behind the front desk, and looked around agitatedly. He froze when he saw Ethan.

Ethan pushed away from the wall and smiled weakly at his lover as the latter marched toward him. "Hey, Joe. I—"

That was as far as Ethan got before Joe engulfed him tightly in his arms.

"Shit!" Joe groaned. He buried his face in Ethan's hair, his hands clenching almost painfully into Ethan's back. "I thought I was going to have a heart attack when the cops called!" He straightened, took hold of Ethan's shoulders, and held him at arm's length while he examined him from head to toe, his hazel eyes blazing with fear and panic. "Are you okay? Did they hurt you?!"

Ethan grimaced. "Well, apart from my pride taking a hit, I'm—" His breath stuttered when Joe raised a hand and gently stroked the pad of his thumb across his swollen lip.

Joe's eyes darkened with anger. "Did those assholes do this to you?"

"I managed to land a few hits before one of them took a swipe at me," Ethan murmured, heat suffusing his body from where Joe was touching him. It never ceased to amaze him how hot he got for Joe the moment he laid a single finger on him.

Joe's jaw clenched when his gaze dropped to the

swollen, red knuckles of Ethan's right hand, oblivious to the direction Ethan's thoughts had just taken. "Fuck."

"Ethan?" someone called out from the other side of the reception area. Ethan looked past Joe to the man heading briskly toward them. The guy slowed as he drew close and acknowledged Joe with a curt nod. "Hey, Joe."

"Asahi," Joe said, nodding back.

Asahi Watanabe was the brother of Ethan's accountant and a detective in the Tokyo Metropolitan Police Department. Ethan and Joe had gotten to know him two years ago, when the detective took the lead in the case of the violent stalker who had shadowed Ethan for months before finally attacking him in the back alley behind *Saron*, the club owned by Joe.

Asahi had happened to be in the area that afternoon when Ethan had called him to ask for his help after the cops brought him, Eveline, and their assailants to the local station.

"You were lucky," Asahi told Ethan with a faint frown. "There was a security camera on the street covering the entrance to the restaurant where you and Miss Claude had lunch. It caught the whole episode and corroborates your versions of events. We won't be pressing any charges against the two of you."

Relief flooded Ethan at the detective's words.

"Good. 'Cause *we* sure as hell want to!" Joe snarled.

Ethan's stomach twisted when he laid a hand on Joe's arm and felt Joe's body vibrate with fury. Although they were blissfully happy in their relationship and had been so for two years, Ethan knew Joe still harbored guilty feelings about the stalker incident that had almost seen Ethan lose his life. For some unfathomable reason, Joe blamed himself for what had happened to Ethan at that time. He'd been incredibly protective of Ethan ever since, so much so there were days when he could be an overbearing ass about the whole thing.

Ethan realized that today's episode must have given Joe flashbacks from the night when the stalker almost raped and killed him. He cursed himself internally. *Shit. Maybe I should have just called Lincoln.*

The station's front doors crashed open once more.

"Speak of the devil," Ethan muttered when a tall man with flashing blue eyes stomped inside the building.

The sergeant at the front desk heaved a weary sigh as he watched Lincoln Hudson walk over to where Ethan stood with Joe and Asahi.

"Where is she?" Lincoln asked tersely as he stopped before them, his back rigid and his hands fisted at his sides.

The door to the interrogation room opened across the way. Eveline walked out ahead of the female detective and froze when she saw Lincoln. The blood drained from her face.

"Linc," she mumbled. "I'm so sorry."

Lincoln swore, closed the distance to Eveline in a handful of strides, and took her in his arms before kissing her passionately. Shock flashed across Eveline's face for an instant before she closed her eyes and fairly melted in Lincoln's embrace, her arms rising to loop around his neck and her fingers spearing his hair to clutch desperately at his head.

The female detective studied the floor pointedly behind them, her ears flushing a bright red. Asahi finally blew out a sigh and cleared his throat.

Lincoln slowly raised his head at the sound. He gazed fiercely at Eveline where she stood in his hold, her expression glazed from their torrid kiss. "I'm the one who's sorry. Shit, I can't believe my father pulled a stunt like that!" He twisted around and looked over at Ethan and Joe, his face full of remorse. "Ethan, Joe, I can't apologize enough for what happened today. I—"

An electronic buzz sounded from the security door on the far right of the reception area. It swung open a second later.

Ethan tensed when the men who'd attacked him and Eveline were led out of a corridor by two uniformed cops. Their assailants' hands were cuffed behind their backs and they both had bloodied lips and bruised faces. The guy who'd manhandled Ethan had a puffy, bloodshot left eye and was walking awkwardly.

Ethan stifled a grimace. *Well, she did kick him in the balls. Twice.*

"Are those the guys?" Lincoln asked in a glacial voice.

"Linc, wait—," Eveline started apprehensively as Lincoln let go of her and stormed across the station.

Asahi straightened and took a couple of steps in Lincoln's direction. "Mr. Hudson, calm—"

Lincoln ignored the detective and halted a couple of feet from the silent pair. "Since I know you'll be talking to the—*senator*," he spat out, "tell my father I have a message for him. If he dares threaten—," Lincoln stopped, his face flushing with rage and his fingers clenching and unclenching at his sides. "No, tell him from this day forward if he so much dares to even *look* at the woman I'm going to marry, there will be hell to pay!"

Stunned silence fell across the station reception in the wake of his words.

Eveline gaped at Lincoln. "Huh?"

"Did Linc just propose?" Ethan hissed to Joe.

"I think so," Joe muttered.

"Did you—," Eveline swallowed convulsively, "—did you say *marry*?!" Her voice rose to a high-pitched squeak on the final word.

Lincoln twisted on his heels and stared at Eveline. "Yes. I want to marry you." He walked back to her, his expression determined, and got down on one knee.

The female detective gasped and covered her mouth with her hands, her eyes bright with ill-contained excitement.

"Shit," Asahi said with a long-suffering expression. "I'm never gonna hear the end of this."

Lincoln took Eveline's limp hands in his own and looked up at her heatedly. "Eveline Grace Forstenberg, will you do me the honor of accepting to be my wife?"

"Forstenberg?" Ethan mumbled, surprised.

"Her birth name," Joe murmured out of the corner of his mouth.

Eveline stared at Lincoln, her eyes wide. She

opened and closed her mouth soundlessly. "No," she finally breathed.

The female detective gasped. The sergeant at the front desk sucked air between his teeth.

"Oh," Asahi said, nonplussed.

Ethan's jaw sagged open. "What?!" he and Joe exclaimed at the same time.

Lincoln blinked at Eveline, his expression similarly dumbfounded. "*Seriously*?!"

Eveline looked dazedly around the police station. "Well, I thought if you were going to propose one day, it would be in a, you know—more romantic location. Like Venice or something." Her face fell, her eyes filling with tears. She sniffed. "With wine and roses. And I wanted a ring, goddamnit!"

Relief flooded Lincoln's ashen face. He rose to his feet and stared at Eveline, his eyes shining with joy. "So, you mean, the answer is actually *yes*?"

"Well, yeah, you big dope!" Eveline whined. She grabbed Lincoln's suit and buried her face in his chest.

Lincoln grinned and stroked Eveline's hair while she sniveled in his shirt. "There, there. I'll buy you ten rings. And a cellar full of wine. And gardens full of roses. I tell you what, why don't I call the pilot and we can get on the jet and fly over to Venice right now?"

Ethan took hold of Joe's hand and smiled goofily at the blubbering woman and the beaming man standing in the middle of the police station, so happy his heart could burst.

CHAPTER EIGHT

"He proposed in a police station?!" Ash Colby said, stunned.

"Yup," Lana Keele said with a grin. "Went down on one knee and everything."

Luke Rutherford smiled faintly next to Ash. "You gotta hand it to the guy. That's pretty original."

Tom Sutherland took a sip of his champagne and rolled his eyes where he sat beside Lana in Luke's private jet. "I'm amazed no one is acting more surprised about *why* they ended up at the police station in the first place."

Lana waved a hand dismissively. "Oh, that's nothing. Ask Ethan about the time Eveline flipped Joe on his back."

"*No!*" Ash gasped with a bark of shocked laughter, his fingers tightening around Luke's where they clasped hands on the armrest separating their seats.

A warm glow filled Luke as he glanced at the young man next to him. It had been a year since he'd moved

Ash in with him from Stanford to Singapore and they'd finally admitted their love for one another, a love that both men had thought doomed from the start and would remain unrequited. Although they'd hit a stormy patch in the first few months of their relationship due to Luke's stubbornness, they were now blissfully happy and settled into their lives as a couple.

Despite Luke's repeated reassurances, Ash had initially been hesitant about being physical with him in public, anxious over whether news of Luke having a gay lover would affect Rutherford Industries, the billion-dollar company Luke had inherited from his father. It wasn't until Luke finally lost his patience one night, took Ash in his arms, and almost kissed the young Colby heir senseless in the middle of a glamorous business social function to make his point clear that Ash finally let go of his inhibitions.

Ash's casual touches, how he leaned into Luke or rested his head on Luke's shoulder, the unconscious way he instinctively reached for Luke's hand when they were next to each other—all of them were precious little signs that made Luke fall deeper and deeper in love with him every day.

"Hmm," Lana murmured across the way. A teasing smile curved her lips as she glanced at Tom. "If it weren't for the fact that we were on their plane right now, I'd say we should leave the room. Luke looks like he's about to eat Ash."

"He always looks like he's about to eat Ash," Tom said bluntly, his gaze moving from Luke to Ash and back again. "I'm surprised the kid can walk most days."

Ash groaned and blushed furiously next to Luke while Lana burst out laughing.

"That's the pot calling the kettle black now, isn't it?" Luke said tartly as he watched the couple opposite him. "I could have sworn I saw the two of you disappear in one of the washrooms at that glitzy party we went to in Shanghai last month and not come out for, oh, at least an hour."

Tom arched an eyebrow, his expression unabashed. "What can I say?" He leaned over and dropped a peck on Lana's left cheek, his eyes shining with tenderness and amusement. "I have a demanding business partner who can't get enough of my body."

"Damn right she can't," Lana said with a wicked grin. She curled her fingers in the back of Tom's head and took his mouth in a scorching kiss that made him grip his armrest hard.

Ash pursed his lips. "Who's eating whom now?"

Luke chuckled. It had been four months since Lana and Tom finally got together. Although their friends had seen the spark of attraction between them from the get go, it had taken a drunken incident one night for Lana to finally realize how important Tom was to her. Their relationship had had about an explosive a start as Luke and Ash's, and it was only thanks to Lana's perseverance that Tom had finally accepted that she truly loved him.

Making Tom a business partner in Keele Industries, the company Lana had inherited from her father and where Tom had worked as her secretary for four years, made sense for those who knew the couple well. Tom was more than qualified for the job and had been crucial to Keele Industries' phenomenal rebirth and rise to success following the company's near collapse at the hands of Lana's uncles.

Rebecca, Luke's flight attendant, poked her head through the curtain separating the main cabin of the jet from the galley kitchen, interrupting his thoughts.

"Wait's almost over!" she said excitedly. "We're landing in thirty minutes."

Ash sighed. "It still can't believe you know more about this gig than we do."

Rebecca made a zipping motion of her fingers across her lips, her eyes twinkling with laughter.

They'd left Shanghai well over an hour ago on their way to the mysterious destination Ethan had arranged for Cam and Gabe's combined bachelor party to take place at for the next two nights. The only instructions they'd been given by Luke's flight crew were what clothes to pack and how long they were going to be away for.

"Oh." Ash's eyes widened when a peninsula appeared beneath the wings of the jet moments later.

Lana leaned across Tom and stared curiously through the port window. She smiled at what she saw. "Nice choice."

The jet soon circled on approach and touched down smoothly on a runway sitting on a wide river delta linked to an island. It turned onto a causeway crossing the sparkling green waters and rolled to a stop opposite a row of private hangars to the south of the airport.

Rebecca opened the cabin door ahead of them as they rose and headed down the aisle. "Have fun!" she said with a grin.

"Thanks," Luke drawled.

A wave of humid heat washed over him when he descended the steps of his jet, the others in his wake. He reached a strip of red carpet lined with purple and yellow flower petals and followed it with his gaze to the open back door of the shiny, black limo some twenty feet away.

The uniformed chauffeur waiting beside the vehicle beamed at them, lifted his cap, and bowed at the waist. "Welcome to Macau."

CHAPTER NINE

Gabe sighed and leaned back against Cam, his gaze on the panoramic views of Cotai, Macau's very own Las Vegas strip, spread out below the balcony of their room. With dusk falling across the city, the vibrant lights of the luxury hotels and casinos made for a colorful backdrop beneath the orange and red streaks splashed across the darkening sky.

They'd landed on the peninsula two hours ago with Ethan, Joe, Eveline, Lincoln, Rhys, and Wade, Lincoln having placed his jet at their disposal for the weekend. That Ethan had managed to keep the location of their bachelor party a secret until the very last moment was a testament to his iron will and sheer stubbornness. Plus, there was the fact that he'd stated rather smugly two months ago that it would take a ridiculous six-figure bribe to get him to spill any beans, a sum everyone knew he could make on the stock market in a handful of days.

Gabe had still been reeling at the incredible setting

his friend had chosen to celebrate his and Cam's upcoming nuptials when they'd been whisked away from the airport by two limos to a resort located a mere ten-minute drive away on the Cotai strip. They were still busy quizzing a grinning Ethan about what he'd planned for them over the next two days and nights when they'd reached their hotel and been greeted by a team of private butlers in the lobby.

"Have fun," Ethan had said with a filthy grin as Cam and Gabe's host took them in the direction of a private lift. "We're meeting here at seven."

Cam and Gabe had entered the elevator under a battery of teasing jeers and whistles and been taken up to the breathtakingly extravagant, split-level penthouse Ethan had booked for them for their trip. From what their butler had told them, Ethan and the others were staying in the equally sumptuous private pool villas located in the hotel's gardens.

"I can't believe he got us the Presidential Suite," Gabe muttered, glancing around their luxurious surroundings once more.

Scented candles and rose petals lined the edges of the indoor pool he and Cam were lounging in. Beyond it was the bedroom where they had just made love.

Cam picked up his flute of champagne from the tray holding an ice bucket with a bottle of Dom Perignon and a bowl of fresh strawberries.

"I gotta hand it to Ethan," he said lazily as he took a sip of his drink. "The kid did good." He picked one of the succulent red fruits, bit half of it, and popped the rest between Gabe's lips.

Gabe let out a sigh as the sweet taste of the strawberry exploded on his tongue. He crunched down on the soft flesh of the fruit before slowly licking the pink juice coating Cam's fingers. Cam tightened his arm around Gabe's waist beneath the water as Gabe flicked his tongue languorously against his skin, Cam's erection pressing against Gabe's butt.

Gabe wriggled his ass and earned himself a curse. He smiled at Cam over his shoulder.

"Considering we just fucked rather spectacularly, I'm not quite sure why you're sporting *that* right now," he said, wrinkling his nose.

"What can I say?" Cam murmured shamelessly. "You inspire me." He kissed the side of Gabe's neck, placed his glass on the edge of the pool, and twisted Gabe around until the latter straddled Cam's lap.

Gabe coiled his arms around Cam's neck as Cam took his mouth in a blistering kiss. A breathy moan rumbled up his throat when he tasted the heady mix of strawberries, champagne, and Cam's own unique flavor. Heat flooded Gabe's body as he slowly drowned in Cam's touch, the intoxicating fragrance of the candles and flowers filling their suite heightening his arousal, his hips gently rocking and rubbing his cock against Cam's erection beneath the surface of the water.

Cam suddenly lifted Gabe off his lap and rose to his feet, his expression feverish with desire. He dragged Gabe out of the pool and hauled him dripping wet across the bedroom and into the en suite bathroom.

"How long have we got?" Cam growled, stepping

inside the walk-in shower. He twisted knobs that sent hot jets pouring down over their heads and across their bodies from all angles, grabbed Gabe's butt, and hitched him up against his body.

"Forty minutes!" Gabe gasped, his arms wrapping instinctively around Cam's shoulders as the latter slid his hands under Gabe's thighs and hoisted them until Gabe's legs were locked firmly around his hips.

"Good," Cam said gruffly, pressing Gabe's back to the marble wall. He positioned the tip of his rock-hard cock against Gabe's twitching hole and entered him in one smooth glide that drew a cry of need from deep inside Gabe's chest.

Gabe clung to Cam and started moving his hips, matching the cadence of Cam's forceful thrusts. Pleasure sparked through him as Cam impaled his sensitive passage repeatedly with his thick shaft, the slap of their wet flesh and Cam's grunts where he nuzzled and nipped the skin of Gabe's throat an erotic music that had Gabe climaxing far too quickly.

Cam carried on fucking him while he came down from his incredible high, his fingers digging into Gabe's flesh where he gripped his ass. His torrid kisses and sinful touch and filthy words soon took Gabe right back up to the dizzy heights of ecstasy until he fell apart once more, his cries echoing above Cam's own animal growls as the latter pulsed and exploded deep inside him, filling Gabe's insides with the hot, sticky evidence of his climax.

The sounds of their ragged breathing were drowned by the sound of the water pelting their bodies as they rested in each other's arms in the aftermath of their explosive orgasms. Cam pulled out and slowly lowered Gabe's trembling legs to the floor, his own body still twitching and shivering with aftershocks of pleasure. He pressed the sweetest kiss to Gabe's lips and murmured the words Gabe never tired of hearing.

"I love you, Gabe."

CHAPTER TEN

"You're late," Rhys Damon said drily when Cam and Gabe stepped out of the elevator fifty minutes later.

Wade looked at his watch where he stood next to Rhys in his tuxedo, his expression triumphant. "Ten minutes." He turned and extended a hand to Joe, Luke, Lincoln, and Tom. "I win. Cough up."

The others grumbled good-naturedly before placing ten-dollar bills in Wade's hand, Ash watching on with an amused smile.

Cam narrowed his eyes as he and Gabe closed the distance to where the group had gathered in the middle of the hotel lobby. "You guys were placing bets?"

Wade pocketed his winnings and linked his hand with Rhys's, a grin splitting his face. "It was Ethan's idea."

Rhys arched an eyebrow at Cam. "He said, and I quote, 'That man won't be able to keep his filthy hands off my best friend for five minutes, let alone three hours.'" His gaze shifted to Gabe. "Judging by how satisfied Gabe looks right now, I'd say he has a point."

Cam sniffed and placed a possessive hand on the small of Gabe's back. "Damn straight, he does."

Rhys chuckled when Gabe reddened beside Cam.

"Where are Ethan and the girls?" Gabe said, glancing around the crowded lobby.

"Ethan's over there, checking on final arrangements," Lincoln said, motioning toward the main entrance. "The ladies are—"

"Right here," someone said from their left.

Eveline and Lana slowed to a stop a few feet from where they stood. The women's faces filled with appreciation as they studied the men critically.

"Holy wow," Eveline added, her blue eyes twinkling as brightly as the beautiful solitaire diamond engagement ring gracing her ring finger.

"You guys sure scrub up nice," Lana said, inspecting their black tuxedos, crisp white shirts, bow ties, and gleaming dress shoes.

"You ladies don't look so bad either," Cam said wryly.

Eveline glanced at her gown and Lana's. "Somehow, I doubt these fine people are ogling *us* right now," she said tartly, indicating the avid stares they were drawing from the hotel guests milling about the lobby. "Not when you guys look like you just stepped out of some kind of glamor shoot."

"Damn." Lana sighed, placed her hands on her hips, and pursed her lips. "We're gonna have our hands full keeping the women—and men—from groping you guys tonight."

"You're exaggerating," Gabe mumbled, his ears flushed.

Eveline grinned, strolled up to Gabe, and ran a hand teasingly down his shirt. "Oh, sweetie. You have no idea how delectable you look right now, do you?"

"I—umm," Gabe said in a flustered voice that made the rest of them laugh.

Cam took Gabe's hand and gave it a slight squeeze. Eveline was right. As far as he was concerned, Gabe was the most gorgeous creature here tonight. It had taken all of Cam's willpower to not strip his fiancé of his formal evening wear and carry him straight back to bed when he'd seen him dressed up to the hilt ten minutes ago, bachelor party be damned.

"Evie, will you quit manhandling the groom?" Ethan berated as he crossed the lobby toward them. He stopped next to Joe and narrowed his eyes at Cam. "It's a good thing I built some extra time into our schedule because a certain somebody can't keep it in his pants." His expression warmed when he took in Gabe's slicked-back hair and immaculate outfit. "Gabe, you look fucking hot. If it wasn't for the fact that I know Joe would castrate me, I would so get it on with you right now."

Joe sighed, hooked a hand behind Ethan's neck, and swooped down to take Ethan's mouth in a kiss that elicited catcalls from the rest of them. Ethan clutched Joe's dinner jacket in a white-knuckled grip and fairly melted into his lover.

"You've had enough fun at our expense, you little tease," Joe growled against Ethan's lips. "So how about you finally tell us what you've cooked up tonight?"

Ethan blinked his eyes open dazedly and licked his lips. "Oh. Hmm. Sure." He turned and motioned to a butler standing to attention close by.

The man came forward and gave Ethan a black velvet tote. Ethan opened it and handed out a smaller bag to each of the couples present.

Cam rolled his eyes when he saw the words emblazoned in shimmering, golden letters on the front. "'Cam and Gabe's Weekend of Sin'? Seriously?"

"'Cam and Gabe's Sex-Filled Marathon' was taken, so grin and bear it, big boy," Ethan said.

Inside each bag was a polaroid camera, several rolls of gambling chips, and a simple, black key card.

Rhys raised his eyebrows when he saw the name engraved on the tokens. "You got us tables at The Venetian?"

"Yup," Ethan said, motioning them toward the main entrance.

"What's the key card for?" Lana said curiously as they headed across the hotel lobby.

"That's for tomorrow night," Ethan replied with a mysterious smile. "Make sure you keep it safe. You're not gonna want to miss what comes with that key card."

Two limos sat waiting at the curb when they stepped out into the humid Macau night.

Ethan rubbed his hands gleefully. "Let's get this party started!"

CHAPTER ELEVEN

WADE SIPPED HIS CHAMPAGNE AND SMILED WHEN LANA fist pumped the air and shouted a jubilant "*Yes!*" a few feet away.

The croupier pushed the gambling chips on the roulette table toward the growing pile in front of the grinning brunette under the faintly disgusted stares of Rhys, Lincoln, Ash, and Joe. At the next table, Ethan let out an excited "Woohoo!" as he won his own game against Luke, Tom, Cam, and Eveline. Like Wade, Gabe had abstained from joining this particular round and was busy taking pictures with everyone's polaroid cameras.

Rhys left the table, climbed the steps of the private, cordoned off area of the casino Ethan had reserved for them, and joined Wade on the main floor.

"That woman has amazing luck for a supposed beginner." Rhys lifted an olive from the tray of snacks on the high table next to Wade and munched on the fruit, a disgruntled scowl still marring his brow.

"I'm surprised you're still hungry after that dinner," Wade drawled as he watched his lover chew. "That Lobster Thermidor just about killed me."

"Well, you know I have a high metabolism," Rhys muttered, licking his fingers clean.

Heat flared inside Wade as he watched the pink flesh of Rhys's tongue dart between his lips.

Why is it that everything this man does turns me on so much?

Although they had been best friends since their college days and business partners for seven years, their relationship only took a romantic turn twelve months ago, after Wade challenged Rhys to a trial period to see if the attraction they felt for one another could turn into something more. Finding out that Rhys had wanted and loved him for over a decade had shocked Wade to the core, and it had taken him a while to realize that he had fallen in love with Rhys a long time ago too. Their affair almost ended following a stupid misunderstanding and it was only thanks to Rhys's friends that Wade had managed to track Rhys down to the mountain cabin where he had taken refuge last Christmas to nurse his broken heart. Convincing Rhys that he was serious about him still ranked as the most challenging thing Wade had ever done in his life. Every day with Rhys since then was a blessing Wade never took for granted.

He captured Rhys's hand presently and squeezed his fingers lightly. "What say we go work out that metabolism of yours somewhere else and help me burn off that ridiculously rich dessert we shared?"

Rhys's baby blue eyes darkened as he studied Wade. He stepped up to him until they stood toe to toe and bit down gently on Wade's lower lip. He let go with a wet pop that sent Wade's blood storming south.

"Why, Mr. Tucker," Rhys murmured against Wade's mouth, "are you proposing we escape from here and go engage in some—," he ran a finger lightly across Wade's crotch and his growing erection, "—risky business?"

Wade swallowed a groan and hooked an arm around Rhys's waist before pulling him tightly against his body. "If by risky business you mean do I want to suck your dick before I fuck you, then yes, that's exactly what I mean, Mr. Damon," he whispered in Rhys's right ear.

Rhys pulled his head back slightly and stared at Wade, his pupils dilated. Wade could tell from the hard bulge pressing against his groin and the way Rhys's breathing had turned shallow and fast that he was as aroused as Wade was right now.

Wade grabbed Rhys's hand and led him through the crowded casino, searching for a place where he could fulfill the filthy promise he'd just made to his lover. He was losing hope they would ever find such a spot when Rhys said, "Over there." Wade followed Rhys's gaze to a narrow, deserted corridor.

They headed down the passage, turned a corner, and found a service elevator at the end. Wade pulled Rhys inside and scanned the cabin for cameras. Satisfied there were none, he pressed the number for a random floor. A soft electronic whirr sounded as the cabin started its ascent.

"Ever had sex inside an elevator before, Rhys?" Wade said, his dick pressing up painfully behind the zipper of his pants as he studied the layout of the compartment and its mirrored walls.

Rhys's eyes widened slightly when Wade turned to look at him. His lips curved in a sultry smile in the next instant. "I can't say I have."

Wade hit the stop button, bringing the cabin to a grinding halt between two floors. "Well, I think you're gonna love it."

He pressed a hand to Rhys's chest, maneuvered him until he had his back pressed against the doors, and dropped to his knees in front of him.

Rhys's cheekbones flushed a dusky pink as he looked down at Wade. Wade kept his gaze locked on Rhys's while he slid his fingers under Rhys's black cummerbund and undid the top button of his pants. He found Rhys's zipper with his teeth and pulled it down carefully over his lover's straining erection.

Rhys sucked air between his teeth when Wade pulled his briefs down and finally freed his cock. Wade's own dick throbbed between his thighs as the musky scent of Rhys's pre-cum hit his nostrils. He dropped a gentle kiss on the wet tip of Rhys's swollen shaft. Rhys let out a shaky moan and grabbed Wade's shoulders.

"Keep your eyes on the mirror, Rhys," Wade purred.

Rhys's head snapped up. Wade gripped Rhys's hips firmly in his large hands and went down on his man while the latter watched their filthy reflection across the way.

Up and down and to and fro Wade bobbed, his tongue and lips working their magic while Rhys shuddered and moaned and grunted above him, fingers digging sharply into Wade's shoulders with every spasm of pleasure Wade delivered.

By the time Rhys released a guttural shout and climaxed inside Wade's greedy mouth, Wade was more than ready to sink his cock inside Rhys's body. He yanked Rhys's trousers and briefs off his legs while the latter still trembled from his orgasm, hooked Rhys's right thigh over his left shoulder, and slicked two fingers with his own spit and Rhys's cum. Rhys arched his back against the metal doors when Wade pressed the tips against his exposed hole.

He relaxed and opened up for Wade as the latter rubbed and teased his twitching rim. Fire licked Wade as he slipped past the inner rings of muscles guarding Rhys's entrance. He pulled back and thrust his fingers inside Rhys's hot, tight channel, mimicking what he very much intended to do with his dick in the moments that would follow.

Wade gritted his teeth and took his time stretching Rhys's opening, knowing if he didn't do so, it would make the act painful for Rhys.

"Wade," Rhys breathed above him, a delicious shiver racing through his body.

"Yes, Rhys?" Wade grunted as he scissored and rotated his fingers in quick, deep jabs that caused the tips to bump against Rhys's prostate.

"*Now!*" Rhys keened softly, rocking his hips against Wade's hand. "I want you inside me!"

Blood pounded through every part of Wade's body as he slipped his fingers out of Rhys. He moved Rhys's thigh off his shoulder, rose to his feet, and palmed Rhys's butt with both hands.

Wade twisted, pushed Rhys against the mirrored wall next to the doors, and lifted Rhys's legs around his hips.

Rhys coiled his arms around Wade's shoulders and locked his ankles across Wade's buttocks, his breaths coming in heavy, rapid pants as he anchored himself securely.

"Eyes on the mirror, Rhys!" Wade growled. He unzipped his pants, freed his straining cock, and guided the tip to Rhys's opening. He pushed in until he was balls deep inside Rhys's body.

Then, with the two of them watching their multiplying reflections in opposing mirrors, Wade fucked Rhys long and hard until they both cried out and exploded in each other's arms.

CHAPTER TWELVE

"AND WHERE DID YOU TWO DISAPPEAR TO LAST NIGHT?"
Ethan said tartly where he stood bathed in the late morning sunlight.

Wade and Rhys strolled up to him and the group waiting outside the hotel.

"We had a private matter to attend to," Rhys said enigmatically.

Wade smiled and hooked an arm around Rhys's waist. "In an elevator." He held up two fingers. "Twice."

Rhys sighed and turned to his lover while the rest of them laughed and ribbed them mercilessly. "So crude, you brute," he muttered admonishingly.

Wade grinned and dropped a kiss on Rhys's lips. "And don't you just love it, you charmer."

They climbed into the town cars Ethan had arranged for their day trip and headed north over one of the iconic bridges that spanned the river estuary separating Taipa Island from the Macau Peninsula.

Ethan had ordered everyone to bring their beach wear and they all wore light summer clothes, the men sporting shorts and T-shirts while the women donned dresses. They pulled into a marina some fifteen minutes later and stopped next to a luxurious sailing yacht.

"Whoa," Ash murmured.

Joe glanced at Ethan as he stepped out of the town car and studied the sleek lines of the vessel and the crew waiting for them. "We're going sailing?"

Ethan smiled. "Yup. We're headed to the outer islands. The chef's doing a beach barbecue for us in a sheltered cove off the beaten track."

It took over an hour for them to sail to the private beach. They had champagne with their seafood barbecue and spent the afternoon swimming and sunning themselves in the cove. By the time they returned to the hotel, the sun was setting over Macau.

"I'm having a light dinner sent to everyone's room in about two hours," Ethan said when they entered the lobby. "We meet here at nine."

Ash groaned and patted his washboard belly. "I don't think I can eat anything else."

Ethan flashed him a wicked smile. "I would have something if I were you." He glanced at Luke. "You're going to need *all* the energy you can muster by the time tonight is over."

Luke narrowed his eyes, puzzled. "And what's that supposed to mean?"

Ethan's grin widened. "Don't forget to bring your black key cards and cameras." He turned to Cam and

Gabe. "As for you two, you'll get picked up from your room, so stay put."

"Why do I not like the sound of that?" Cam murmured with a suspicious frown.

Eveline came up to Ethan while the rest of them disbanded. "So," she said, her blue eyes sparkling mischievously as she cocked her head to the side, "I've been doing a bit of research about that key card. Is it what I think it is?"

Ethan stifled a chuckle and gave her his most haughty stare. "And what do you think it is?"

Eveline rose up on tip toes and whispered something in his ear. Ethan bit his lip to stop the laughter threatening to escape him.

Eveline's eyes widened at his expression. She grinned. "You filthy fucker."

"You think the rest of them are going to like it?" Ethan asked, a sliver of doubt flashing through him. He'd hesitated a lot before planning the events of the second night of Gabe and Cam's bachelor party.

Eveline laughed. "They're gonna love it! I predict Cam will put up a fight. But once he sees what the rest of the night has to offer, he's going to be super thrilled."

Relief flooded Ethan. "Good. I want everyone to have a good time."

"Trust me, Linc and I will be having a *very* good time," Eveline said with a saucy wink. She blew him a kiss over her shoulder as she strolled toward where Lincoln stood waiting for her.

Ethan was still smiling when his cell buzzed in his

shorts pocket. He pulled it out and stiffened when he saw the text message lighting up the screen.

"You coming?" Joe said.

Ethan's heart thudded inside his chest as he looked at his lover. "You go ahead," he said in a light tone. "I just have to finalize a couple of things." He waited until Joe had disappeared in the direction of their private villa before hitting dial on his cell. Someone picked up after a couple of rings. "Hi, this is Ethan."

"Mr. Skye? I have some news for you and Mr. Anderson," the man at the other end said.

Ethan swallowed, a sick feeling swirling in the pit of his stomach. He clenched the cell tightly. *This is it.* "Yes?"

"I found them."

CHAPTER THIRTEEN

GABE FIDGETED NERVOUSLY WITH HIS CUFF LINKS AS HE waited for Cam to join him in the suite's hallway. Ethan had texted him three hours ago. When Gabe read the message, his legs had almost given out under him.

He sat down shakily on the edge of the bed and read Ethan's words over and over again while the sound of running water echoed from the bathroom where Cam was taking a shower.

Ethan: Hey, you still there?

Gabe realized Ethan was waiting for his response. He tapped out a quick reply.

Gabe: Yes.

Ethan: He told us not to get our hopes up, so I was kind of resigned to the fact that this would come to a big nothing.

Gabe: I know.

Ethan: I'm in shock. And a little bit scared. This is really going to happen.

Gabe worried his lower lip with his teeth as he read Ethan's text.

Gabe: They might say no.

Ethan: I know. I hope they don't. It's four weeks until your wedding, so we have plenty of time to talk to them.

Gabe: Yes. And Ethan?

Ethan: Yeah?

Gabe: Thank you.

Ethan: Love you, Gabe. Have fun tonight!

Cam walked out of the bedroom presently, his hands at the base of his throat as he finished knotting his bow tie. Gabe stilled and looked at the man he was going to marry in a month's time, his heart stuttering in his chest.

God, he is so beautiful.

"Does this look okay?" Cam said, stopping in front of him.

Gabe lifted his fingers to Cam's tie. Not that he needed to adjust it. It was perfect as it was, just like the man who wore it.

"It does now," he said, pressing a kiss to Cam's lips.

Cam smiled. "That's sneaky."

Gabe chuckled as Cam wrapped an arm around his waist and pulled him close for a searing kiss. They were interrupted by the sound of the suite's doorbell.

Gabe reluctantly wrenched his lips from Cam's. "That must be our pick up."

Cam arched an eyebrow. "We could pretend nobody's home."

"Behave," Gabe said in a fake rebuking tone as he headed for the door. He opened it to find two police officers on the threshold.

❧

LINCOLN LOOKED AT HIS WATCH. "ARE WE EARLY OR IS Ethan late?"

"He's late," Tom muttered. "By eight minutes, on my count."

Joe frowned faintly. "He's said he'd only be a moment. He was right behind me. Maybe I should go check on him."

Eveline grabbed Joe's arm as he turned to retrace his steps to his and Ethan's villa. "I wouldn't do that, Joe."

Joe stopped and raised an eyebrow at Eveline. "What? Why?"

"Somehow, I get the feeling Ethan is exactly where he wants to be right now," Eveline replied.

Lincoln narrowed his eyes at his fiancée. He knew that teasing look in her eyes. "Evie, is there something you need to tell us?"

Evie grinned and shook her head. "Nope."

Lana sucked in air, her green eyes widening. "You know what's happening tonight, don't you?"

Eveline bit her lower lip to stifle a giggle. "I hope everybody's got their key card."

A flash of intuition darted through Lincoln as he beheld Eveline's gaze. "Oh." A slow smile curved his lips. "If this is what I think it is, this is gonna be fun."

"What's gonna be fun?" Rhys said, puzzled.

A commotion near the main entrance drew everyone's gaze. A group of tall, muscular police officers entered the hotel and headed across the lobby toward them. The beefy guy in the lead halted a few feet from where they stood and scanned their group with a stern expression.

"Are you the party of Mr. Ethan Skye?" he said.

Luke stiffened. "We are."

"What's going on?" Wade said with a frown.

The burly cop ignored Wade's question. "Please come with us."

A muscle jumped in Tom's cheek. He stepped in front of Lana. "Not until you tell us what the hell is—"

Eveline placed a hand on Tom's shoulder. "It's okay."

She strolled up to the cop. "I'm guilty. Please arrest me." She smiled and held out her hands.

"*Huh?*" Lana gasped.

"What the—" Ash stammered as the cop removed cuffs from a pouch at his waist and secured Eveline's wrists.

Lincoln raised a hand. "I'm guilty too."

"Hang on a minute—" Luke growled as another cop cuffed Lincoln.

"Hey, guys." Rhys stared at the cops. "I would do as these kind gentlemen say."

Wade gaped at Rhys. "Why the—"

"Look at their uniforms, Wade," Rhys said, his expression relaxing. "Left epaulette."

Wade peered at the cops' outfits. His eyes widened. "Does that say—"

Lana covered her mouth and snorted. "Oh God! This is gonna be hilarious!"

Joe groaned. "That little minx!"

THEIR RIDE IN THE BACK OF THE FAKE POLICE VAN TOOK just under twenty minutes.

"Please step this way," the burly cop said when the vehicle doors opened at the other end.

They came out into the warm Macau night. Joe looked around. They were in a narrow alley behind a building. A red, metal door opened to their left. They were escorted past a shadowy figure, navigated corridors painted in vivid reds and purples, and were finally led into a large, dimly-lit space.

Joe blinked as his eyes slowly adjusted to the gloom. The room was about the size of *Saron*'s floor space, his club in Tokyo. A swanky bar took up most of the wall space to the right. At the opposite end of the room, beyond low tables and leather chairs arranged in discrete clusters, was a raised, semi-circular stage. They could hear the sound of faint activity behind the purple velvet curtains pulled closed across it.

The cops removed their cuffs just as a woman approached them from a doorway to the left of the stage. She was dressed in red heels, black fishnet stockings, and a lace-trimmed ruby corset with a frilly burlesque skirt.

"Hello. My name is Isabella. Welcome to the club," she said with a smile. "I hope you'll enjoy what we have in store for you tonight." Music boomed from the speakers lining the walls, a steady, drumming beat that seeped into the bones. "Please take a seat."

She led them to the row of tables that had been arranged in a half circle in front of the stage. Champagne bottles chilled in ice buckets on stands next to each one. More hostesses in burlesque outfits appeared in the gloom and poured their drinks as they settled in the chairs.

Joe glanced at Eveline where she sat with Lincoln at the next table. "Are Cam and Gabe—"

Before he could finish the sentence, the music suddenly dropped in volume.

"Ladies and gentlemen, welcome to Wicked!" a voice boomed from behind the velvet curtains. "Before we start the show, we have a word from our sponsor tonight."

The curtains shivered as someone came through.

Joe stared at the slightly nervous looking blond in the formal evening suit smiling sheepishly at them.

"Hi, everyone," Ethan said. "So, for our final night in Macau celebrating Cam and Gabe's upcoming wedding, I wanted to treat all of you to something really special. Tonight's party consists of two parts. First, we have a show. After that, each couple will be escorted to, umm, a private room I've personally selected for them." He winked. "I hope you're gonna love what's inside."

"*Woohoo*!" Lana shouted. "Does that mean I get to tie Tom up?"

Tom sighed next to her and sipped his champagne with a faint smile.

Ethan laughed. "I'm sure you'll find plenty of toys to have fun with."

Lincoln let out a loud catcall. "Either get off the stage or strip, Skye!"

Eveline rose, cupped her hands around her mouth, and chanted, "*Strip, strip, strip!*"

"Not happening, Evie," Ethan said with a smug smirk. "The only one who gets to see me naked is Joe."

Heat coiled inside Joe's belly when Ethan met his gaze.

"And now, for the show!" Ethan stepped off the platform and joined Joe at their table.

"You are in so much trouble," Joe growled. He hooked a hand behind Ethan's neck as he took his seat and pulled him close for a passionate kiss. Ethan gasped as their tongues clashed.

"The good kind?" Ethan mumbled.

Joe bit down on Ethan's lower lip. "Definitely the good kind."

Ethan shivered slightly at the promise, his eyes darkening to a stormy green. The music got loud again. The velvet curtains finally parted. Joe smiled.

The cops who'd arrested them were spread out across the stage in formation, their faces relaxed in easy smiles.

Seated on leather stools in the middle of them were Cam and Gabe. They were in their formal evening wear and had their hands cuffed behind their backs. They'd also been blindfolded. Gabe's cheeks were flushed and his shoulders shook while he struggled to stifle his laughter.

The burly guy in charge of the male strippers masquerading as police officers walked to the front of the stage and grinned at them. "Are you guys ready to have some fun?" He grabbed his crotch and pumped his hips in a suggestive motion.

"*Hell yes!*" Ash shouted.

The burly cop winked at Ash. "Oooh, I like you! You're feisty." His gaze shifted to Ash's left. "Don't worry, grandpa. I'm not about to steal your boy toy."

Everyone howled with laughter while Luke spluttered out a shocked, "Grand—*grandpa*?!"

Two of the cops removed Cam and Gabe's

blindfolds. Gabe blinked. His eyes widened as he took in their surroundings. A chuckle escaped his lips.

Cam stared at Ethan. "You're a dead man, Skye."

The show began.

CHAPTER FOURTEEN

Luke slipped the black key card into the lock of the private room and opened the door, one arm around Ash's waist where the latter rested heavily against him. He thanked the hostess who'd brought them to the suite, guided Ash inside, and turned to close the door.

Ash moved from his hold and stumbled a couple of steps forward.

"Whoops!"

He giggled, crossed the floor unsteadily, and flopped backward on the bed dominating the elegantly decorated red and black suite, oblivious to what lay around him. "Hey, Luke, is it me or is this place spinning?"

Luke smiled faintly at his lover. "You're drunk."

Ash pushed up on his elbows and directed a faintly mutinous scowl at him. "No, I'm not!" he announced haughtily. He hiccuped and fell back on the bed.

Luke chuckled.

The sexy, provocative male striptease show Ethan

had arranged for Cam and Gabe's bachelor party had ended a short while ago. As the rest of them whooped and stamped their feet and clapped their hands to the rousing finale, Cam and Gabe had sat grinning in the middle of the stage, both clearly enjoying the display of brawny, near-naked men writhing and dancing around and against them. Although Cam had scowled when half the strippers decided to give Gabe a seriously hot lap dance.

Anticipation stirred through Luke as his gaze swept the playroom Ethan had chosen for them. A range of chic leather and wood furniture specially designed for sex and BDSM play dotted the floor and suspended from metal beams in the ceiling. Lining the shelves and hooks on the walls were toys and tools designed to stimulate and titillate. Floor-length mirrors stood in strategic places around the space, where they would heighten the visual experience of whatever was taking place inside the playroom. Artful drawings of men and women engaged in various explicit sexual acts completed the erotic ambience.

Luke had visited a few sex clubs and dungeons in the past to see what it was all about. Though he'd found the experience interesting and had enjoyed the activities he'd participated in with both male and female partners, it never formed an essential aspect of his own sex life. It wasn't something he and Ash had ever explored during their relationship to date either. Luke hadn't even been sure of Ash's thoughts on the topic until they'd come here tonight.

The heated glances Ash had cast at him during the

strip show and the flush of color painting his cheekbones since he'd realized what Ethan intended for them afterward had told Luke everything he needed to know about his lover's feelings concerning their current situation. Luke wasn't sure if Ash had drunk too much champagne to garner his courage for the night ahead, or because he'd gotten carried away by the buzz and excitement of the club's atmosphere.

Well, whichever reason it was, I best get him a little sober before we get down to business.

As he pondered which of the toys on the walls Ash would want to play with first, Luke strode to the mini fridge sitting at the far end of the room. He found bottled water inside and was busy untwisting the cap off one when a buzzing noise reached his ears. He twisted on his heels and froze at the sight that met his eyes.

Ash was sitting on the side of the bed and examining the pink dildo vibrating furiously in one of his hands with a faint frown. With the other, he picked a small black square from a box lying next to him and popped it in his mouth.

Luke swallowed a groan, his dick stirring at the sinful sight of Ash and the dildo. "What are you eating?"

He marched around the bed, lifted the box out of the young man's reach, and inspected the contents. It was chocolate. He read the writing on the back of the carton and sighed when he saw the list of ingredients.

"Ash, these are aphrodisiacs. Where did you find them?"

Ash indicated the open nightstand with the dildo still dancing in his hand. Luke put the box down and was busy checking what else lay inside the drawers when he heard more munching. He turned around.

Ash had stuffed his mouth with more chocolate and was chomping on them with a delighted expression.

"For the love of—" Luke stepped to the bed and snatched the box away. His eyes widened as he stared inside. "Hmmm, Ash. How many of these did you just have?"

Ash shrugged. "Don't know," he mumbled with a full mouth. He swallowed, wiped a hand clumsily across his chocolate-coated lips, and paused when he saw the sticky streak on his skin.

Luke's cock throbbed and swelled when Ash carefully licked the sweet remains of the chocolate off his flesh.

Ash's gaze arrowed in on the box in Luke's hold. "I want more," he said in a stubborn voice.

"No, you don't." Luke turned, headed inside the bathroom, and hid the box of aphrodisiacs on top of a cabinet. He returned to the playroom, tilted Ash's chin with one hand, and pressed the rim of the bottled water to his mouth. "Here, have this."

Ash frowned at his command. "You're a such a party pooper," he grumbled.

"You won't be saying that in the next hour or so," Luke drawled. "Now, drink."

Ash sighed and did as he was told, his long lashes fluttering low over his cheeks. The water spilled slightly from his lips and wet his skin and Luke's fingers as he took deep, hungry gulps.

The sight of Ash's Adam's Apple bobbing sensuously in his throat and the way he hollowed his cheeks as he sat there in his immaculate thousand-dollar tux following Luke's order sent a sudden shiver of need down Luke's spine.

Jesus, he's so fucking sexy. I can't believe he's really mine.

Ash finished the bottle. Luke was leaning away to reach for the cap when Ash suddenly grabbed his hand and licked the wet trails on his fingers. He lifted seductive, steel-blue eyes and met Luke's stare unblinkingly. A wicked smile curved his moist lips.

"There you go. *Grandpa.*"

Lust slammed into Luke with the force of a hammer at Ash's sultry, aroused look. He cast the bottle into a bin by the nightstand, spread Ash's knees wide with one powerful leg, and stepped inside the cradle of Ash's thighs.

A gasp escaped Ash's lips when Luke speared his hair with his fingers and tugged, causing Ash's neck to arch back. Blue clashed with amber as they locked gazes, their breathing shallow and fast.

Luke's heart thudded with feverish anticipation as he leaned toward Ash.

"Grandpa, was it?" he murmured an inch from Ash's mouth. "I think you're gonna be grateful for Grandpa's stamina in a little while, Ash." He nipped at Ash's lower lip with his teeth and smiled when Ash shuddered in his grip.

"And why is that?" Ash panted, pupils dilated so wide his eyes were almost black.

"Because once those aphrodisiacs kick in, you're gonna be begging me to fuck you over and over again." Luke took Ash's lips in a slow, deep kiss.

Ash moaned and bucked his hips off the mattress as their tongues danced together.

Luke reluctantly broke the kiss a moment later. "Why don't we start with appetizers?" he said huskily.

He ran a finger lightly down Ash's exposed throat and chest, skittered over his six-pack and belly, and paused when he bumped against the healthy erection straining behind Ash's zipper.

Ash cursed when Luke opened his pants and freed his dick.

Luke palmed the twitching, flushed shaft, let go of Ash's hair, and lowered himself to his knees between Ash's legs. Ash watched him unblinkingly as he closed his large hands on his thighs and spread them wider. Ash clutched the bedsheets and dropped his head back as Luke opened his mouth and took him inside. Ash's lips parted on a long, low moan that had Luke's own dick doing press-ups in his pants as he started blowing him.

By the time Luke sank his cock deep inside Ash's body, he'd brought Ash to two screaming orgasms and the aphrodisiacs had started to work their magic. He pinned the writhing, sweaty, flushed young man beneath him to the bed and started fucking him the way he knew he loved to be fucked. Fast and hard. Slow and deep. On his back and then on all fours.

They used some of the toys, including the pink dildo, and even tried out a couple of the other fittings in the room.

All the while, Ash moaned and panted and cried and begged for more, his sensitized skin, nipples, and dick twitching at Luke's every touch and kiss and the leather and silk items Luke stimulated him with, his hole squeezing and spasming and milking Luke's hard shaft hungrily as the night wore on.

CHAPTER FIFTEEN

Ethan groaned and closed his eyes briefly as another dizzying wave of pleasure shot through him from his ass. The sounds he made were muffled by the black ball gag in his mouth. Leather creaked as he unconsciously tugged on the restraints around his wrists and ankles.

He was strapped to a frame suspended from the ceiling of the playroom, his arms and legs spread wide open and secured with enough slack for them not to hurt where he hung several feet off the floor.

Joe sat in a purple leather chair opposite him, left ankle atop his right knee, his elbows resting loosely on the armrests. He'd stripped out of his suit jacket and undone his bow tie. The ends hung loosely around his neck, framing his partially open shirt and his exposed, tanned chest.

In his right hand was a small, black remote.

Joe's eyes glittered with a dark desire as he stared at Ethan naked and trussed up in front of him. A smile curved his lips, faint yet filled with so much animal hunger Ethan couldn't help shuddering. Joe pressed one of the buttons on the remote.

The black leather butt plug wedged in Ethan's lubed-up hole vibrated once more for long unholy seconds, causing him to curse and moan in pleasure. Sweat dripped off his nose while he panted and tried to catch his breath after the delicious torture ended. He glanced down his body to his straining, flushed dick trapped in the leather ring enclosing the base of his erection. Beneath it, another leather ring cupped his balls snuggly and linked to the butt plug by a thick rubber bridge.

Ethan had never worn a cock and ball ring before. To say that he was loving the experience was an understatement. He'd never had so many dry orgasms as he'd done in the hour since they'd been inside the playroom.

Ethan hadn't been sure what to expect when Joe walked in behind him and saw what lay inside the black and purple suite Ethan had selected specially for them. Joe used to be an escort for Eveline's clubs and had indulged in bondage before with clients, so none of it would be new to him. And although they'd tied each other up during sex and used toys, they'd never engaged in full BDSM play before.

Joe locked the door and carefully examined the room and its contents, his hazel eyes growing inscrutable. He walked over to a wall bearing a variety of leather and silk floggers and fingered one of them.

"Nice," he murmured.

Butterflies swamped Ethan's stomach where he stood in

the middle of the room; he felt strangely nervous all of a sudden. He was well aware he was a novice compared to Joe when it came to some of the items around them. He glanced at the leather restraints hanging from the suspension beams to the left and swallowed. His gaze clashed with Joe's in the next instant.

Joe held Ethan's eyes and slowly walked over to the contraption. He touched one of the padded cuffs. "Is this what you want to try, Ethan?"

"Umm," Ethan mumbled, his ears warming.

Joe watched him for a moment. He closed the distance between them, tilted Ethan's chin up slightly with one crooked finger, and repeated the question. "I said, is this what you want, Ethan?"

Hot and cold shivers suddenly raced through Ethan as he finally grasped what it was he was reading on Joe's face. Joe was beyond fucking turned on by all of this; most of all, he seemed to be loving the idea of Ethan in those restraints. Ethan swallowed convulsively as the fire burning in the hazel eyes opposite him licked his skin and threatened to consume him.

Joe leaned in and brought his lips to Ethan's ear. "I would never do anything to hurt you," he said in a low, gravelly tone that made Ethan's heart stumble a beat. "If we do this, it will only be about pleasure. Yours and mine."

That was all it took for Ethan to finally admit his filthy wish. "Yes," he breathed.

Joe's finger moved to another button on the remote. He studied Ethan unblinkingly and pressed it.

Electricity buzzed through Ethan as the butt plug started to work its magic in a different way, pulsing and throbbing in a heady rhythm that made the nerve endings lining his sensitized rim and passage sing to attention. He whimpered and grunted as pressure built deep inside his belly and balls, dark, intense waves that indicated he was nearing another mind-blowing climax. His toes curled and his fingers clenched.

Joe brought him right to the brink of the orgasm before turning the vibrator off. Ethan squeezed his eyes shut and whimpered, his belly tensing and quivering while his butt cheeks squeezed the leather intruder inside his passage, trying to stimulate himself over that dizzying verge.

Although Joe had promised he wouldn't hurt him, the way he'd teased and edged him was pretty damn close to the sweetest torment Ethan had ever suffered. Not knowing when Joe would allow him to climax or when he'd reel him back from tipping over into the delicious fall only ramped up the pleasure tenfold. And Ethan knew it wasn't just him who was relishing the exquisite play they were engaged in right now.

Clothes rustled up ahead. Ethan blinked his eyes open. His pulse hammered wildly in his veins as he watched Joe uncross his legs and spread his thighs wide open where he sat in the leather chair opposite him.

Joe held Ethan's gaze and unleashed the enormous erection in his pants. Ethan's hole spasmed around the butt plug as he stared at the pre-cum pearling the head of Joe's cock.

Fuck. I want to lick that so bad.

As if he'd read his mind, Joe swiped his thumb across the creamy drops and sucked on it slowly with a lewd, wet sound, his cheeks hollowing enticingly while he moved his finger in and out of his lips.

That was all it took for Ethan to come. He bit down on the leather ball gag and let out an indistinct shout as his passage and dick pulsated violently. A thin jet of cum finally escaped his swollen, trapped shaft and splashed across his chest. By the time Ethan recovered from the spine-tingling orgasm, Joe was on his feet.

He palmed his hard cock and started rubbing himself as he closed the distance to Ethan, his hazel eyes ablaze with lust.

Ethan panted and trembled when Joe stopped in front of him. Joe's gaze swept his body, burning him everywhere it landed. From his head down to the cock and ball ring framing his groin and the attached butt plug, and all the way up his legs and arms to the shackles holding his ankles and wrists prisoner.

A moan ripped out of Ethan's throat when Joe leaned down and licked the trail of cum on his chest. He furrowed the thick, pink flesh and flicked the tip across Ethan's nipples, causing him to swear and jerk against his restraints.

"I don't think I gave you permission to come, Ethan," Joe murmured against his sweat-slicked skin, his fingers still busy on his own glistening dick.

Ethan's heart thundered against his ribs as he looked into the hazel eyes boring into him. They both knew what was coming next.

Ethan fisted his hands and cried out against the ball gag when Joe activated the butt plug once more. Joe reached under Ethan's body, gripped the base of the device, and pulled down gently.

Light exploded behind Ethan's eyes as the broadest part of the toy came into contact with the rings of muscles guarding his entrance once more. Then, Joe closed his lips on the head of Ethan's shaft.

The room faded as Joe started sucking and deep throating Ethan's cock while he thrust and rotated and pumped the vibrating plug inside Ethan's hot, wet hole, stretching him and teasing the sensitive nerves of his rim.

A buzzing noise filled Ethan's ears as the exquisite orgasm surged through him, tightening his balls and stiffening his spine. Higher and higher it built, rising and receding in agonizing, electrifying tingles while he moaned louder and louder against the ball gag.

A white haze enveloped Ethan's mind and body when he exploded inside Joe's mouth a moment later.

He was dimly aware that he was shuddering and shaking and jerking against his restraints as he surfed and crested the violent waves of ecstasy ripping through him while Joe hungrily swallowed his cum. The sounds he was making reached him from a distance—long, guttural animal cries and grunts. He wondered fuzzily whether it was really him making those noises.

He felt Joe remove the butt plug.

It was replaced by something else. Something thicker. Longer. Hotter. Harder.

Ethan's breaths came out in hard, fast pants as he finally drifted down from the dizzying heights Joe had just taken him to. He blinked dazedly and stared at the man who had his dick now wedged deep inside him.

"Have I told you how fucking beautiful you look when you come?" Joe said in a voice thick with desire. He drew his hips back before flexing them forward.

Ethan gasped at the sensation of Joe's shaft plunging deep inside him.

"All of it," Joe murmured reverently, fingers clenching on Ethan's butt where he held him. He fixed him in position and started fucking him, his movements slow and hard, matching the unhurried cadence of his wicked words, driving Ethan steadily out of his mind all over again.

"From the way your eyes glaze over just before it hits you." Joe pulled out. "And your cheeks and ears and neck go bright pink as you fight the pleasure until the very last moment." He pushed back in with a wet slap of flesh that drew a tortured moan of pleasure from Ethan's throat and sent a spark of white light flashing across his vision.

"To how your nipples stiffen into hard little nubs I want to bite." Joe undid the ball gag and dropped the leather item on the floor.

Ethan swallowed and licked his lips, unable to tear his eyes from the man in front of him. The man inside him. The man possessing him with an erotic mastery he had never before experienced. He gasped when Joe withdrew his hot shaft until only the broad head stretched his entrance.

Joe lowered his gaze down Ethan's flushed, sweat-slicked body. "And I love the way you clench and tighten your belly." He raised his head and took Ethan's mouth in a deep kiss while he thrust back in, bumping Ethan's prostate. His lips swallowed the moan ripped from deep inside Ethan's chest. "Just that alone is enough to make me shoot my load, Ethan. It makes me wonder what it's like inside there, where I know you feel your pleasure the most. Does it look the way I think it does? The way it feels to me?"

Joe brought his mouth to Ethan's ear and bit the lobe gently as he pulled out again. "Like a star getting bigger and brighter with each movement of my dick inside you?"

Electric tingles rippled through Ethan when Joe plunged back inside him with a powerful motion.

"A hot, tight ball of energy dying to explode? To go supernova?"

A harsh grunt left Joe's lips as he pulled out again.

Ethan trembled, his pulse racing in his veins as he stared into the dilated hazel eyes opposite his. He could tell Joe was starting to lose control from the way he was tensing his jaw.

The leather restraints creaked as Joe slammed home once more, air leaving him in a low hiss. "To consume everything in its path in blinding waves of pleasure that make you forget who and where you are?"

The way Joe's fingers suddenly dug into Ethan's butt cheeks told him his lover had finally reached the limits of this game. Joe clenched his teeth and started pounding Ethan's ass harder and faster, sending fiery jolts of pleasure through Ethan's hole.

"I hope it does, Ethan," Joe groaned, sweat pearling

his upper lip. "Because that's the way it feels to me whenever I'm with you. Like there's a star exploding inside me. Taking me over. Destroying me. Remaking me. Just for you. Just for this."

Joe buried his face in Ethan's throat and pressed a kiss to his heated skin. Ethan's heart soared as the man he loved surrendered completely to his carnal instincts and fucked him the way he really wanted to—wildly, passionately, without restraint, like an animal claiming his mate.

Branding him.

Owning him.

Marking him in all the colors of their love.

CHAPTER SIXTEEN

Lincoln grinned at Eveline.

"I gotta say, I could get used to that look."

Eveline glanced at the red leather dominatrix outfit kissing her alluring curves like a second skin. She ran her hands down her waist and hips. "You like it?"

Lincoln nodded where he sat naked on a bondage chair, his sizable cock already at full mast between his thighs. If it wasn't for the fact that his arms and legs were strapped down, he'd be unzipping the front-to-back crotch of the traffic-red PVC catsuit Eveline had just slipped into and be balls deep inside her.

The playroom Ethan had chosen for them was not dissimilar to the special-access VIP rooms in Eveline's clubs. The one in Tokyo was where he and Eveline first had sex, and that night still remained one of the most memorable ones of Lincoln's life.

It was Lincoln who'd suggested Eveline take on the role she used to play in the past when they came to the playroom a short while ago.

That of a professional dominatrix.

Although they took turns taking the lead during sex, Lincoln knew Eveline thoroughly enjoyed surrendering control to him when they were in bed. He'd always been curious about what she would be like in complete control. And truth be told, quite a little turned on by the idea.

Eveline strolled to the table next to the chair, her black stilettos clicking sensuously against the floorboards. She tapped a finger against her lips while she examined the tools laid out on a surgical tray.

"What should we start with first?" she murmured teasingly.

She trailed her fingers over a range of whips and floggers before lovingly caressing a string of blue, teardrop shaped silicone beads on a flexible rod with a finger hook at one end.

Lincoln's ass clenched as he stared at the anal beads.

Eveline chuckled. "Don't worry, I'm just kidding. I —" She stopped, her pupils widening as her gaze dropped to his erection.

Lincoln bit back a groan. There was no hiding the fact that it had just gotten noticeably bigger.

Eveline raised her eyes to Lincoln's face. Color painted red flags across her cheekbones. "Fuck. Your dick seems to like that idea." She glanced at the anal beads, excitement brightening her face. "Do you want me to use those on you?"

Lincoln shifted in the chair and cleared his throat. "I, umm, might be amenable to trying them out."

Eveline sucked air between her teeth, her

expression that of someone who just got all her Christmas gifts six months early. Her gaze shifted to the row of specialized tools suspended from hooks on the wall to her left.

Lincoln tensed when he saw what she was staring at.

"Now, let's not get carried away, Evie," he said warningly, his hands fisting under the leather restraints binding him to the chair.

Eveline pursed her lips. "So, that's a no to the strap-on dildo?"

"Hell, no!" Lincoln stated vehemently.

Eveline sighed and picked up a whip. "How about this?"

Lincoln eyed the leather rod. His gaze shifted to the flogger next to it. "That one looks more…interesting."

A wicked smile curved Eveline's lips. "Good choice."

That was when Lincoln knew he was in trouble.

By the time Eveline finished tormenting every erogenous zone of his body with the bondage tool and some ice cubes from the fridge in the corner of the playroom, Lincoln was breathing fast and his cock was leaking pre-cum almost continuously. And when Eveline slowly, carefully prepped his ass with lube and slipped the anal beads inside, Lincoln cursed and dropped his head back, so close to shooting his load at the insane sensation of being penetrated he only managed to hold back his orgasm by the barest thread.

A tiny wave of disappointment flashed through him as his passage adjusted to the intruder inside him. Bar a feeling like he needed to bear down and push it out, the anal beads felt strangely inoffensive. He'd expected them to be more…*pleasurable.*

Eveline must have read his mind as she smiled at him then. "Don't worry, babe." She slipped a condom on his dick, undid the crotch zipper of the catsuit, and straddled his lap. "It's not what they do while they're just sitting there." She gripped his shoulder with one hand, clasped his twitching cock, and guided it to her sex. "It's what you do *with* them."

Lincoln hissed as Eveline came down on him, her passage swallowing his dick in hot, tight, velvety heat. She was so wet for him he slid inside in one smooth glide. He tightened his pelvic muscles instinctively and gasped when his ass suddenly tingled with a spark of pleasure.

Eveline grinned at his shocked expression. "That's it, sweetheart." She leaned forward and nibbled his right earlobe with her teeth. "You gotta squeeze those little suckers," she whispered. "Like this." She tightened her inner muscles around him.

Lincoln cursed and pumped his hips reflexively. The beads moved inside him and generated another jolt of electricity that matched the one burning through his cock.

Eveline pressed her heels against the floor and started riding him, rising until his cock was teasing her folds before punching down again, her mouth parted on hot, sexy pants. She kept her left hand on his right shoulder and leaned back slightly before reaching for the zipper at the top of the catsuit.

A red haze of lust swamped Lincoln's vision as

Eveline slid the metal down over her chest, freed her naked breasts, and started touching herself, her fingers rubbing and pinching her erect nipples while she bit and chewed her lower lip, low hums of pleasure rumbling up her throat.

Lincoln held Eveline's passion-glazed eyes as he gripped the armrests of the chair and started thrusting up to meet her downward plunges, his hole rhythmically grasping the small, hot balls inside his back passage with every punch of his hips.

"*Fuck!*" Lincoln gasped as the tingles of pleasure radiating from his dick and ass merged and pooled deep inside his belly.

Eveline's moans grew into cries as she accelerated her pace. Sweat beaded her face, and her chest and face grew flushed with pleasure when the first ripples of her climax trembled through her sex.

Lincoln's entire body stiffened deliciously as his own orgasm raced down his spine and arrowed in on his dick, balls, and ass. Movements growing erratic, he tilted his hips and plunged harder and faster into Eveline while she melted and shuddered and came around him, her convulsions squeezing and milking his throbbing shaft.

Just as Lincoln's body detonated with the first exquisite wave of his climax, Eveline reached behind her, hooked her finger around the ring at the end of the anal beads wedged in his ass, and started pulling them out slowly one by one.

Lincoln let out a harsh shout at the intense pulses of pleasure their exit created in combination with his orgasm. He cursed and gasped and grunted as his cock spurted jet after jet of cum inside the condom while the beads slipped out, so much so he wondered dimly if his dick would ever stop squirting.

He collapsed against Eveline a dizzying moment later, blood roaring in his ears while his heart pounded violently in his chest, his face slick with sweat.

"Holy shit," Lincoln mumbled once he got his breath back.

Eveline giggled where she still straddled his lap. "That good, huh?"

"It was fucking unreal," Lincoln admitted fervently.

Eveline blew a stray strand of blonde hair off her face and glanced at the strap-on dildo with a hopeful gleam in her eyes.

Lincoln groaned. "Let's not transition from handgun to bazooka in one night, shall we? I don't think my virgin hole could take the torture."

Eveline drew in a sharp breath. "*Oh!* Does that mean you'd be open to—" She flexed her hips against his in a sexy motion that demonstrated what she so clearly wanted to do with the naughty leather device on the wall.

Lincoln eyed her as haughtily as a naked man who'd just had his ass masterfully played with could hope to do. "That's a subject for another day. Now, untie me so I can take you to that bed and have my wicked way with you."

Eveline grinned. "Yes, sir."

CHAPTER SEVENTEEN

"*Ouch!*" Tom murmured.

"Sorry!" Lana mumbled.

Tom glanced at his reddening nipples before studying the woman straddling his body.

Lana was wearing a gauzy little black number she'd found in the wardrobe of the playroom Ethan had chosen for them. The skimpy nightdress displayed her naked breasts, pert nipples, and the tiny scrap of silk barely covering her sex in ways that was making Tom regret having ever agreed to be tied down in the first place. As it was, he was lying butt naked on the bed with his arms and legs bound to the posters by leather shackles.

Lana worried her lower lip and frowned faintly at the nipple clamps in her hands, as if doing so would elucidate the mystery of how she should use them.

"Maybe you should let me continue," Tom said, his engorged cock pulsing with a spasm of anticipation at the thought of how he would use those clamps on Lana.

"No way!" Lana protested. She shifted back a bit and rocked her butt against his sensitized shaft. "I called dibs on tying you up, remember?"

Tom sighed. *At this rate, she's going to make me come before I'm inside her.* He put on his most convincing expression. "I'm kinda worried about the damage you might do if you keep playing with those toys the wrong way."

Lana gave the nipple clamps a suspicious look. "You are?"

"Yup," Tom said. "What if you cut off the blood circulation to my nipples? I mean, I could lose them. I'd be—," he bit his lip and just about managed to keep a straight face, "—Nippleless Man."

Lana gaped at him, her eyes rounding. "You're kidding, right?!"

"I've heard stories," Tom said.

Lana's expression grew suspicious. "From whom? You don't seem like the BDSM club kinda guy."

"From friends," Tom countered vaguely.

Lana's expression didn't change.

"If you let me go, I'll do that thing you love," Tom offered temptingly. "You know. *That* thing."

Lana's eyes darkened to jade and her breathing accelerated. She glanced over her shoulder at Tom's straining dick.

"Okay," she finally relented, her voice breathy with excitement.

Finally!

Tom waited until Lana had freed him before he grabbed her by the waist and flipped her on her back. "Gotcha!"

She laughed and gazed at him where he crouched on all fours above her, her wrists trapped in his hands. "Oh, yeah? Whatcha gonna do now you got me, Mr. Sutherland?"

Her eyes roamed his body while she waited for his reply, her dilating pupils telling him she was loving what she was seeing. Tom swallowed a groan when she stared unblinkingly at his dick and bit her lower lip, a hungry look pasted across her face.

He arched an eyebrow. "Why, I'm gonna ravish you, Miss Keele." He leaned down and tugged on her right earlobe with his teeth. "*Every* part of you."

Lana shuddered when his breath washed over her skin.

Tom grabbed a condom from the box on the nightstand, found some lube in the drawer, and dropped both items on the sheets next to him. He took Lana's mouth in a scorching kiss that had her arching off the bed and started to work his way down her body, his hands caressing her curves ahead of his mouth. He nibbled on her breasts through the nightdress, rolled his tongue around her nipples until she was moaning and gasping, and kissed a fiery trail down her trembling belly to her crotch.

Tom's cock throbbed when the musky scent of Lana's arousal hit his nostrils. He closed his mouth on the material covering her sex and sucked.

Lana cried out and bucked against his face. Tom let

go of her wrists, cradled her hips in his hands, and found her clit with his tongue.

She called out his name in high-pitched keens as he teased her mercilessly, alternating between lapping and flicking her sensitive nub and cupping it with his lips and sucking. Tom peeled the nightdress up over her belly, hooked a finger in the edge of her damp panties, and pulled them to the side, exposing her sex.

Lana cursed when he slipped two fingers inside her wet heat and started thrusting. She twisted her hands in his hair and pushed his face against her body, silently begging for more.

Let's get you off so we can both enjoy what comes next, kitten.

With that thought in mind, Tom used his mouth and fingers to bring Lana to her first climax of the night. She came in long, low moans that made his cock pulsate with hunger, her knees pressing against his shoulders, her sex clamping down around his digits in rhythmic contractions that pulled them inside her body. She collapsed back down languidly on the bed a moment later, her lips open on fast, hard pants, her face rosy with pleasure.

Although Tom had never seen anything as sexy as Lana in the midst of coming, he had to admit that her post orgasmic look came a close second. He slipped her panties off her long, lithe legs, propped a pillow under her butt, and hooked her ankles over his shoulders, his movements growing uncontrolled.

He wanted inside her now.

Lana gripped the bedsheets and looked down her body to where he crouched between her legs. Tom held her feverish gaze and dropped a kiss full of promise on the silky skin of her left thigh. He flashed her a filthy smile, parted her butt cheeks with his hands, and dipped down to flick the tip of his tongue against the twitching pucker of her ass.

"*Fuck!*" Lana groaned.

Yup, that's what I'm going to be doing soon enough. Fucking this tight little hole.

Tom took his time prepping Lana's ass with his tongue and lubed-up fingers before flipping her on her front. She rose on her hands and knees and looked at him over her shoulder, her hair tumbling sexily around her face, her eyes dark with passion.

Tom's heart pounded violently against his ribs as he rapidly sheathed his straining dick and spread a liberal amount of lube over his shaft. He positioned himself behind her, spread her butt cheeks with one hand, and guided the head of his cock to her ass.

Lana hissed as he pressed against her, probing the tight folds of her entrance. Tom clenched his jaw and slowly nudged the tip past the slick rim. He waited for her to adjust to the penetration before carefully pushing through the tight rings of muscles quivering and spasming around his shaft.

Lana let out a sensual groan as she absorbed the sting and burn of his penetration.

Tom stilled when he was fully wedged inside her. He leaned down and pressed a kiss to her trembling back, his pulse throbbing in his veins and cock. "You okay?"

"Yeah," Lana breathed. She looked at him over her shoulder. "It feels good. Tight, but good." She squeezed her back passage and smiled when he cursed out loud. "Let me have it, Tom," she murmured sexily. "Let me have all of you."

Tom gnashed his teeth, gripped Lana's hips, and withdrew his cock until only the head parted her opening. He punched back in with a grunt.

"*Yes!*" Lana cried out, her hands twisting in the bedsheets. She rocked her hips and danced back impatiently against him, matching the rhythm of his hard thrusts as he set the pace of their love making.

Pleasure flashed through Tom in rising, electric tingles. His breath hitched when his gaze dropped to the source of the intense sensations building up inside him. Even though he'd seen it all before, he never tired of watching his cock move in and out of Lana's most sinful part. However much he relished making love to Lana the conventional way by fucking her luscious pussy, Tom had to admit doing her in the ass brought its own kind of thrill. He'd been delighted to discover that Lana got as much of a kick out of it as he did when he introduced her to the dark pleasure of having her back passage plundered by his dick a few months past.

Too soon, Tom felt his orgasm start to gather in a tight band at the base of his spine. He reached forward, twisted a hand in Lana's hair, and tugged gently until she rose up on her knees against him.

Lana moaned sultrily when he pressed his lips against the side of her neck. She arched her head to the side to give him better access and reached back to grab his hips while he continued pumping into her from behind.

Tom's balls tingled as he inhaled the heady scent of sweat and sex enveloping them. He cupped Lana's lush breasts with his hands and pinched her nipples, his thrusts growing faster and harder.

"*Oh God!*" Lana gasped.

An incoherent cry left her lips with her next breath as he skimmed a hand down her body and dipped his fingers in the folds of her sex. He teased the sensitive area around her clit until she begged him to touch her. He finally relented and rolled and rubbed the engorged nub just the way she liked it, knowing she was seconds from climaxing from the shivers rippling through her. A harsh grunt tore out of him when she finally exploded against his hand, her passage constricting his dick to the point of pain, her lips open on loud cries and moans.

Tom wrapped his arms around Lana's sweat-slicked body, buried his face in her neck, and rocked his hips erratically against her ass, his orgasm welling up inside him in savage waves while she convulsed deliciously around him. He let out an animal shout as he came seconds later, the pleasure storming through him so fierce he saw stars.

It was a while before awareness returned and the sounds of his and Lana's harsh breathing echoed in his ears. Tom blinked dazedly and realized he'd pushed Lana down on the bed at some point in the last minute and was lying on top of her, his cock still wedged snuggly in her ass. He slipped out carefully, discarded the condom, and rolled her over before lying back down on top of her, his head cradled on her chest.

Lana curled her fingers in his hair and pressed a kiss on top of his dark curls. "That was fucking awesome."

Tom didn't have to look up to see she was smiling. As he did practically every day since he and Lana had gotten together, he thanked whichever God it was who'd finally fulfilled the unrequited love he'd had for the woman in his arms. That she belonged to him, truly belonged to him, was a gift he cherished more than anything in this world.

"What are you thinking?" Lana asked quietly.

Tom's lips curved in a faint smile. It was spooky how she could tell when something was on his mind. He kissed her right breast and raised his head to gaze at her. "I was thinking how much I love you."

Lana's eyes darkened with emotion. "How come you can still slay me with those words, even though you've said them to me hundreds of times before?" she said huskily.

She cradled his face gently in her hands and took his mouth in a slow, sweet kiss. Tom inhaled shakily as he absorbed the emotions she projected with her touch and her lips.

"Hey, Lana?" he murmured throatily when the kiss ended.

"Yeah?"

"Wanna fuck again?" Tom arched an eyebrow and nudged his hardening cock suggestively against the damp folds of her sex.

Lana grinned and wrapped her arms around his neck. "Always."

CHAPTER EIGHTEEN

"So, did everyone enjoy last night?" Ethan asked with a saucy grin.

Wade looked at Rhys across the dining table where they all sat having brunch the next morning in Ethan and Joe's villa. They were flying back home that afternoon. "We sure did," he murmured.

The memories of the sexy, filthy things he and Rhys had done to one another in the club's playroom the night before washed through Wade all over again when his lover's lips curved in a seductive smile.

"Yup," Rhys said, his baby blue eyes shining with mischief as he gazed at Wade.

A low groan sounded from the end of the table, where Ash sat nursing a cup of coffee next to Gabe.

"I'm never drinking again," the Colby heir declared, his face pale.

"Well, no self-respecting bachelor party would be complete without at least one person getting thoroughly wasted," Cam drawled.

Luke came out of the villa's kitchen and plonked a Bloody Mary and a large glass of water next to Ash. "Here, drink up."

Ash eyed the cocktail with suspicion before taking a careful sip. He choked and coughed before grabbing the water and downing half of it. "How much tabasco sauce did you put in there?" he wheezed once he got his breath back.

"Plenty," Luke said sternly. "You're not leaving this table until you drink all of it."

Ash grumbled something under his breath before doing as he was told.

"Like a mother hen," Lincoln muttered teasingly next to Eveline.

"Well, that stripper did call him Grandpa," Tom said with a grin.

"I don't need that from you two misters 'I-fucked-my-girlfriend-so-hard-she-can-barely-walk-this morning,'" Luke said tartly as he took his seat next to Ash.

Eveline propped her elbows on the table and arched an eyebrow at Luke. "Jealousy is an ugly thing, Luke."

"It is," Lana concurred. "Besides, the one struggling to walk this morning is Ethan."

An affronted expression replaced the grin on Ethan's face "I am not!"

Cam turned to Joe while the others chuckled. "Is there something you need to share with us, Joe? I mean, is everything okay, you know—," he waggled his eyebrows, "—with Little Joe?"

Joe smiled lazily at Cam. "Little Joe is fine, Cam. I'm

more worried about how bright and perky Gabe looks this morning. I expected him to be worn out."

"Well, sex is like a pick-me up for this guy," Cam explained while Gabe flushed beside him. "So, the livelier he appears, the harder it means I—"

Gabe covered Cam's mouth with his hand and hissed, *"For Christ's sake, shut up Cam!"* his face bright red.

"What?" Cam mumbled from behind Gabe's palm with an innocent air, his gray eyes dancing with mirth.

Wade and the others laughed at Gabe's at once loving and exasperated expression as he scowled at his fiancé.

CHAPTER NINETEEN

CAM CAREFULLY LIFTED GABE'S ARM OFF HIS CHEST AND tucked it next to the pillow. Gabe stirred, his lashes fluttering briefly against his cheeks. A smile came unbidden to Cam's lips as he watched his lover settle back into a deep sleep.

Nearly a month had passed since their trip to Macau. Cam could hardly believe they were getting married in less than a week. He rose from the bed and padded barefoot to the kitchen, too restless to sleep.

It was Friday night and both he and Gabe had left work late as they finalized their business commitments before their upcoming trip. They were leaving Tokyo on Sunday morning on Lincoln's private jet for their flight to Molokai. Luke, Ash, Lana, and Tom were joining them at Lincoln's resort on Sunday night. Everyone had taken the week off to relax in the sand and sun before the wedding on the following Saturday. Cam and Gabe would stay on for another week in

Lincoln's private villa at the resort for their honeymoon.

Cam took a bottle of water from the fridge and strolled over to the bay windows overlooking the terrace that wrapped around his and Gabe's condo. Tokyo sparkled like a multi-colored jewel before him, still buzzing with life despite the late hour.

A soft sigh left Cam's lips as he drank from the bottle and gazed at the bustling city. He'd never been one for being sentimental about the places where he'd lived before, but he had to admit to being in love with the one he'd called his home for the last few years. It was where he had been the happiest he'd ever been in his life to date. Not just because that's where he'd been reunited with his best friend after nearly two decades. Or met the man he would come to cherish more than his own life. Cam would happily stay in Japan for the rest of his life and he hoped Gabe felt that way too.

A tiny frown marred his brow in the next instant. He hesitated before strolling to the coffee table and picking up his cell where he'd left it there some hours ago. He brought up a number and tapped out a text.

Cam: You up?

The reply came almost instantly.

Joe: Yeah. Just wrapping up some last-minute things at the club before our trip. What's up?

Cam paused before replying.

Cam: Is Ethan with you?

Joe: No. He's gone home already.
What's wrong, Cam?

Cam pursed his lips.

Cam: I think Gabe and Ethan are having
an affair.

Cam's cell rang in the next seconds. He cursed, put it on vibrate, and took the call.

"Are you drunk?" Joe snapped in his ear.

"No, I'm not," Cam muttered. "Don't you find it suspicious how much time they've been spending together lately? And how they're constantly sneaking around behind our backs? Oh, and they suddenly stop talking if one of us walks in on them?"

Joe muttered something rude under his breath. "Look, I get you may be suffering from pre-wedding jitters, but trust me when I say that there is no way in hell Gabe would ever cheat on you. That man worships the ground you walk on. And Ethan loves my dick too much to want another man's inside him." He paused. "Besides, I don't even want to think about who would top whom in a scenario where Ethan sleeps with Gabe."

Cam smiled at that. He had to admit he couldn't either. "Yeah." He sighed. "I know you're right. But I can't help feeling they're up to something. I've never known Gabe be so secretive."

"It's probably to do with the wedding," Joe said. "Speaking of which, I've written my best man speech."

Cam groaned. "You'd better not embarrass me with tales from our youth."

Joe chuckled. "You mean like that one time we snuck out of the children's home and went to check out those prostitutes hanging on the corner of the block a mile away?"

Cam narrowed his eyes. "Yeah, like that kind of shit."

Joe continued, unrelenting. "Oh, and how one of them thought you were sixteen, dragged you in a back alley, and practically French-kissed an orgasm out of you?"

Cam cursed under his breath. "That's exactly the kind of shit I don't want you to talk about, Joe."

"Don't worry your pretty little head, Cam," Joe drawled. "I won't be mentioning *that* night."

Cam grimaced and rubbed the back of his neck awkwardly. "You mean the night we swore never to speak of again for as long as we live?"

"Yup," Joe said, his voice full of suppressed mirth. "That one."

"You told Ethan about it?"

"No," Joe said. "You told Gabe?"

"Nope," Cam replied. "I think it would be best if we never revealed the, er, details of that night to them. I mean, technically, nothing happened."

"But it almost did," Joe said.

Cam scowled. "Don't remind me, you brute. I can't believe you tried to push me down."

"I can't believe you tried to do the same to me," Joe countered drily.

"Yeah, well, despite what you said, height doesn't matter when it comes to fucking," Cam said.

"I think I have a few inches on you in places other than just height, Cam," Joe said.

Cam grinned. "You fucker."

"Right back at you."

Cam ended the call and looked out into the night. He knew deep down inside that Gabe loved him to death and would never cheat on him. But he couldn't deny that Gabe was definitely hiding something from him. Cam could see it from the way he'd catch Gabe watching him from time to time, his expression at once guilty and happy, as if he was nursing a secret.

Well, whatever it is, I'm sure he'll tell me eventually. A smile danced across Cam's lips as he recalled all of the naughty things he and Gabe had done in the sex club's playroom, that second night in Macau. *Or I could tease it out of him.*

CHAPTER TWENTY

"ETHAN, YOU SEEN MY SUNGLASSES?" JOE CALLED OUT from the bedroom.

"I gotta go," Ethan murmured hastily into his cell where he stood on the balcony of his and Joe's condo. He paused and smiled. "I can't wait to meet you too."

Ethan ended the call just as Joe appeared in the lounge. He turned, slipped the phone inside the rear pocket of his jeans, and strolled toward his lover.

"Weren't they in your tennis bag? You had them when you played Cam last weekend."

Joe dropped a quick peck on Ethan's lips. "You're a genius."

Ethan grinned as he watched Joe head back into their bedroom. He hoped he'd successfully masked the excitement coursing through him; there were only a few days left until the plan he and Gabe had been working on for the last two months would finally come to fruition.

His cell rang in the next instant. It was Evie.

"You two had better not be having sex up there," she said when he answered. "We're in the limo outside your building."

Ethan sucked air between his teeth. "Just give me five minutes to finish blowing Joe."

A series of groans echoed in his ear.

"You're on speaker, asshole!" Cam shouted in the background.

"Great," Lincoln muttered next to Eveline. "Now I'm gonna be imagining *that* the whole ride to the airport."

"Fuckers can't keep it in their pants," Rhys said somewhere close by.

Eveline's laughter bubbled through the speaker. "You hear that? Now hurry on down here!"

They left Tokyo within the hour. By the time they reached Molokai and were chauffeured over to the resort, it was nearly ten in the evening local time.

"Whoa," Ethan murmured as their limo pulled up in front of the main hotel building.

"Like it?" Lincoln said with a smile as they stepped out of the vehicle into the balmy night air. Bell boys came to collect their cases while they stood admiring their surroundings in the gentle glow of the flame torches and lanterns that lined the resort's driveway and forecourt.

"What's not to like?" Joe said. "It's stunning, Lincoln."

Eveline grinned at Lincoln and slipped her hand into his. "Even though we've been here a few times, I still think it's the most beautiful place I've ever seen, Linc."

Set on forty acres of lush, tropical grounds fronting a pristine white beach and a crystal-clear lagoon, Lincoln's resort consisted of one central building that housed the administrative offices, the main reception area, and two bars. Spreading out from it like the limbs of a starfish were two hundred single and two-story bungalows, with the beachfront ones having their own private pools, hot tubs, and outdoor showers. In addition to the individualized suites and villas, the resort boasted eight restaurants, six bars, a variety of swimming pools and natural rock pools, two golf courses, tennis courts, a five-star spa, a state-of-the-art fitness center, and several luxury yachts moored at a private pier for day trips around the island. The resort's incredibly successful grand opening a few months ago had made the business news even as far away as Tokyo.

Although the hotel specifically didn't cater to weddings, Lincoln had agreed to let Cam and Gabe have theirs at the venue and had restricted room bookings for the week they would all be there. As such, they would have the place mostly to themselves.

They bumped into Luke, Ash, and Tom in the lobby.

"Hey," Luke said as they hugged and shook hands. "This place is amazing, Lincoln." He dipped his chin at Gabe, Rhys, and Wade. "You guys did a great job on the place."

"Well, it was mostly Gabe," Wade said.

Cam smiled proudly at his fiancé. Though Damon

& Tucker had done the interior design for Lincoln's resort, it was Gabe and his team who'd spearheaded the entire project.

"Where's Lana?" Eveline said, looking around curiously.

Tom grimaced. "She was feeling a bit peaky so I put her to bed when we got here."

Lincoln frowned slightly. "We have a doctor on site if you think she needs to see one."

"Thanks, but I think she'll be okay," Tom said with a faint head shake. "It's probably just jet lag. She doesn't do well on long-haul flights."

They chatted for a bit before heading off to the beachfront villas they'd been assigned for their stay.

Ethan's eyes widened as he entered his and Joe's one-story bungalow. "This place is gorgeous."

They checked out the beautiful master bedroom with its en suite granite bathroom. Beyond a chic lounge and dining area were sliding doors leading onto the deck overlooking their private outdoor pool and lava rock shower.

Joe looped his arms around Ethan's waist from behind as they stepped out into the warm night. "It sure is that."

They stood looking out over the dark Pacific Ocean in comfortable silence, the sound of surf crashing onto the pale beach a short distance away merging with the song of crickets from the nearby bushes and palm trees.

"It's been a long day," Joe finally murmured against Ethan's head. "We should go to bed."

"Hmm," Ethan said with a soft sigh. He turned in Joe's hold and wrapped his arms around Joe's neck. "Carry me there?" he murmured teasingly against Joe's throat.

A gasp left Ethan's lips when Joe suddenly stooped and swung him up into his arms, princess-style.

"I spoil you rotten, you know that, don't you?" Joe said with a low chuckle as he carried Ethan through the villa to the bedroom.

Ethan laughed when Joe dumped him on the bed. Heat flashed though him in the next instant when Joe climbed onto the mattress and crouched above him on all fours. Ethan tugged his lower lip between his teeth and reached for the bottom of Joe's T-shirt.

"That doesn't look like a sleepy face," Joe drawled as Ethan peeled the material up and over his head.

Ethan grinned, drew Joe's zipper down, and slipped his hand inside Joe's jeans to palm his stirring cock.

Joe groaned. "Definitely not a sleepy face," he mumbled, leaning down to kiss Ethan.

CHAPTER TWENTY-ONE

"This is the life." Eveline sipped the cocktail in her hand and sighed as she looked out over the sparkling lagoon a few feet away. A breeze blew in from the ocean and cooled her warm skin.

It was the second morning of their stay at the resort. With their wedding five days away, Gabe and Cam had gone off to meet with their wedding planner to ensure the final arrangements were in place for Saturday.

Lincoln lifted his head where he lay face down on a sun lounger next to her. "Hmm, babe? I think you should pace yourself with those. Barry has a mean hand when it comes to dishing out the vodka."

Eveline reached over and patted Lincoln's thigh. "Worry not, my sweet. I'm alternating them with those killer fruit shakes of his."

"I'm pretty sure I saw him pour booze in the blender when he made those too," Luke muttered from his sun lounger.

Eveline squinted at the large, chilled glass on the table next to her. "Really?"

"Yup," Ash said. "Some kind of rum." The young Colby heir had acquired a beautiful tan since they'd been at the resort and his honey skin was now a nutty bronze.

"Please stop talking about alcohol," Ethan groaned from where he sat on a blanket in the shade behind them. He was lying between Joe's legs where the latter read a book, his back against a tree.

"Oh?" Rhys tipped his sunglasses down the bridge of his nose and arched an eyebrow at Ethan where he sat on the edge of his lounge while Wade applied sun tan lotion to his back. "Is someone regretting his drinking game from last night?"

Eveline grinned. Wade chuckled.

"Told you she could drink you under the table," Joe muttered to Ethan, his eyes still on his book.

"You're supposed to be taking my side, you know," Ethan grumbled.

"I would if you weren't so stubborn," Joe said. "Besides, she gave you plenty of fair warning."

"She did," Luke said.

"Yup," Ash nodded.

Eveline laughed at Ethan's expression. Movement to the right drew her gaze. Lana appeared on the beach, a hat holding her hair securely in place and a willowy white dress hanging loosely on her frame.

"Hey, how are you feeling?" Lincoln said as she joined Ethan and Joe in the shade.

Lana's lips twisted in a brief grimace as she sat down carefully on the blanket. "A bit better."

Concern flooded Eveline as she studied Lana's pale expression. "You don't look better. You sure you don't want us to get the doctor for you?"

Lana shook her head and bit her lip. "No. Whatever this bug is, it tends to be worse in the morning for some reason. I'm usually fine by the afternoon."

Eveline stiffened. She shared a glance with Lincoln. His eyes had just widened too.

"Lana, honey, how long have you been feeling queasy for?" Eveline said gently. She realized she wasn't the only one suddenly staring at Lana. Everyone else was too.

Lana frowned at them. "Hmm, about a week now. Why?"

Rhys rubbed the back of his neck awkwardly. "Are your, umm, boobs sore?"

Surprise widened Lana's eyes. She flushed. "Well, now that you mention it—"

Luke sighed and swung his legs over the side of his sun lounger, his expression pained. "Okay. Since I've known you the longest, I'm gonna come out and ask the question everyone is thinking right now. Lana, when was your last period?"

"Seriously, you guys," Lana spluttered, "what the hell kind of line of questioning is—*Oh!*" She froze in the next instant, her eyes rounding like saucers as she finally grasped what they were trying to tell her. She covered her mouth with her hands. "Holy. Fuck," she mumbled hoarsely.

"Holy fuck what?" Tom said as he joined them, two soda pops in hands. He stopped and frowned as they all stared at him, a shocked Lana included. "Why are you guys looking at me like that for?"

⁂

"Holy fuck," Tom murmured, his heart pounding in his chest.

He stared at the pregnancy test in Lana's hand. It was the third one they'd done in the past half hour and all three were unanimously positive.

Tears suddenly pooled in Lana's eyes.

Tom's chest twisted with a jolt of pain. He wrapped Lana gently in his arms where he sat beside her on the edge of the bathtub and kissed her forehead. "Hey, hey," he hushed against her hair, "it's alright. We'll figure it out."

Lana shook her head. "These aren't sad tears," she said in a wobbly voice. She raised her eyes and met his stunned gaze. "These are happy tears."

A dizzying wave of relief flooded Tom then. He hadn't been sure how he felt about the possibility of Lana falling pregnant so soon into their relationship as a couple; even though they'd known each other for years, they'd barely been together five months. Although they'd spoken about kids, it was all related to a distant hazy future, hence why he always used a condom and Lana was on the pill.

Now that they were sitting there in the bathroom at the resort doctor's office, three positive pregnancy tests in hand, Tom couldn't deny the breathtaking happiness flowing through him. He inhaled shakily, too overwhelmed to speak for a moment.

"So, you want the baby too?" Tom finally said in a trembling voice.

Lana nodded, her green eyes sparkling. "Of course." She pressed a hand carefully to her flat belly. "He or she is a part of you. Of us." She lifted her other hand to Tom's face and caressed his cheek tenderly. "It's a given that I would want someone who is the physical proof of our love."

Tom's vision blurred with his own tears. He took Lana's lips in a sweet kiss before leaning down and pressing his mouth to her belly. "You hear that, kid? Your mama and I can't wait for you to get here."

Someone pounded heavily on the bathroom door.

"Hey, we know you guys are having a moment in there, but, seriously, how long does it take to pee on a stick?" Ethan said loudly from the other side.

Lana chuckled and wiped her tears away as Tom rose and strode over to the door. He opened it to find Ethan with one fist raised to knock again.

"Well?" Ethan asked impatiently.

The others stood behind him, faces similarly expectant. Gabe and Cam were among them, Ethan having gone to find them to share the incredible news.

Tom grinned and took Lana's hand in his own as she joined him. "We're pregnant."

The room erupted in loud whoops and cheers as everyone congratulated them.

Eveline rushed inside the waiting room, her face flushed. "What did I miss?"

"Tom knocked Lana up," Ethan said with a beam. "Where'd you go?"

"*Yes!*" Eveline squealed, fist pumping the air. She rushed over to hug Lana and Tom, tears gleaming in her eyes. "And I went to get this from Tom's bag." She placed a small black velvet box in Tom's hands and kissed his cheek.

A hush descended across the waiting room.

Tom swallowed nervously. He read the encouragement blazing in Eveline's eyes, took a deep breath, and got down on one knee in front of a stunned-looking Lana. "I know it's a bit cliché to be doing this right now, but I've had this for a while and was going ask you the question at Christmas." He opened the box and exposed a beautiful solitaire diamond ring.

Eveline grabbed Lincoln's hand, a goofy expression on her face. Gabe's smile widened as he looped an arm around Cam's waist.

"This belonged to my grandmother," Tom said, his pulse racing madly as he looked up into Lana's jade green eyes. "She bequeathed it to me when she passed away, to give to the woman I wanted to marry one day. I knew that woman was you for a long time, but I never thought I would have the chance to actually give it to you one day."

Tears overflowed Lana's eyes and coursed down her face.

And there, surrounded by their closest friends and

three positive pregnancy tests, Tom finally said the words he'd wanted to say all his life to the woman in front of him.

"Lana, will you do me the honor of agreeing to be my wife?"

A dreamy smile lit up Lana's face. "The honor would be mine, Tom," she said in a choked voice. "The honor would be mine."

Tom wiped his wet eyes with the back of his hand before slipping his grandmother's engagement ring on Lana's finger. He climbed to his feet and chuckled when she launched herself at him and kissed him hard while everyone around them clapped and cheered.

"Wow, this wedding bug is catching," Rhys said teasingly. "Better be careful." He looked at Eveline. "The pregnancy one might be catching too."

Lincoln studied Eveline with a thoughtful expression. She smiled, rose on her tip toes, and pressed a kiss to his lips. "Everything in its own time, Monster Meat. Everything in its own time."

CHAPTER TWENTY-TWO

G ABE GLANCED ANXIOUSLY AT HIS WATCH AS HE WAITED on the deck outside his and Cam's villa. It was finally time.

Cam came out of their bedroom and joined him. "I gotta say, a walk is exactly what I need right now," he said with a heavy sigh. "That wedding rehearsal was nerve-racking. What time are we meeting everyone for dinner?"

Gabe smiled as Cam took his hand and led him out onto the sand. "Seven."

They headed out along the beach, the sun a giant yellow orb slowly sinking toward the horizon to their right.

"You having regrets?" Gabe said teasingly.

"Never," Cam said fervently. "I would do that shit a hundred times over if it means I get to legally call you my husband as of tomorrow."

A wave of happiness surged through Gabe at Cam's

words. After months of debate, they'd finally decided what names they would put on their marriage license.

The beach was nearly deserted, which Gabe knew it would be at this time of day. When they reached the meeting point he'd chosen, Gabe stopped and pulled on Cam's hand.

Cam halted in his tracks and turned to look at him quizzically. "What is it?"

Gabe took Cam's other hand in his own. He looked down at the matching rings gleaming against their tanned skin and inhaled shakily.

This is it.

Gabe looked up and met Cam's curious gaze unblinkingly. "There's something I've been meaning to tell you. Something I've been hiding from you for the last two months."

Cam's eyes darkened. "Finally," he muttered. "You know, you really had me worried—" He stiffened suddenly, his gaze locking on something behind Gabe. He glanced at Gabe with a bemused expression. "If this was your surprise, you really didn't need to hide it from me."

Gabe twisted on his heels. His jaw dropped when he saw the three figures heading toward them from the resort grounds.

"Umm," he mumbled between numb lips. He glanced at Cam, shock reverberating through him. "No, this isn't—"

"Hi, Gabe," Melissa Anderson said with a small smile as she stopped a few feet from where they stood.

She hesitated before coming up to Gabe and rising on her tip toes to kiss his cheek.

Gabe's parents stopped just behind her.

Gabe stared at his family. "I—what—" He swallowed nervously. "I don't understand. What are you doing here?"

"We're here for your wedding, of course," Cathy said adamantly. She strode over to Gabe and hugged him tightly. "I'm sorry, Gabe. For everything." Her voice shook as she buried her face in Gabe's chest.

Gabe wrapped his arms around his mother, his heart thudding wildly against his chest. Never in a million years had he imagined that his family would turn up to his and Cam's wedding. He met his father's slightly aloof stare over his mother's head.

"Congratulations on your upcoming nuptials," George said stiffly.

Melissa sighed. "Dad," she said in a warning tone. "We practiced this."

George frowned before huffing out a heavy sigh. "Alright, alright. I'm sorry for being a stubborn asshole. You boys are welcome to visit anytime you want. After all, you're family now." He directed the latter words at Cam. "As long as you don't tell us about your sex life, I will agree to keep an open mind about—" He waved a hand vaguely at them.

"Practically had to pry his skull open with a crowbar," Melissa said to Gabe and Cam in a theatrical whisper that made Gabe smile.

Cam cocked his head to the side and studied his

future father-in-law with an amused expression. "It's a deal. And we'll hide the vibrator when you come visit us in Tokyo."

Gabe groaned while his sister and mother laughed.

"Relax, George," Cathy said at her husband's flabbergasted expression. "It's not as if he's proposing to stick it up your ass."

A bark of laughter left Cam's lips. Gabe and Melissa gaped at their mother.

Cathy shrugged at her children. "What? I've been reading up on things. So, how exactly does one find a man's prostate?"

"*Mom!*" Gabe gasped.

Melissa and Cam were doubled over at the waist and howling with laughter while George stared open-mouthed at his wife.

That was when Gabe saw the person he'd agreed to meet up with at this very spot. His pulse accelerated as she came down the beach toward them, a yellow summer dress billowing around her large figure, her face rosy from the heat.

"Mom, Dad, Mel?" Gabe mumbled, glancing at his family. "Can we catch up with you in a while? I have to stay with Cam for this."

Melissa and Gabe's parents looked curiously at the grandmotherly figure who stopped a few feet from them. The older woman's eyes were bright with an unnamed emotion as she stared unblinkingly at Cam.

"Sure, Gabe." Cathy smiled at the newcomer and led her husband and daughter back up to the resort.

The woman in the yellow dress came up to Gabe and pressed her lips to his cheek. "My, you are even more handsome in person than on that computer of mine. The screen really did not do you justice."

Gabe flashed a wobbly smile at her. "I'm so glad you made it."

"Gabe?" Cam said, puzzled. He looked from the stranger to Gabe and back again.

Gabe took a deep breath and turned to Cam. "Okay, here goes. That secret I was just telling you about? It wasn't my parents coming to our wedding, Cam." He lifted a hand and caressed Cam's face gently. "Two months ago, Ethan approached me with a wild idea. One that he'd already put into motion before we went to the States to meet my family. You see, Ethan and I hired a detective agency to look into your past and Joe's."

CAM STIFFENED. HE FELT THE BLOOD DRAIN FROM HIS face as he stared at Gabe. "What?" he mumbled hoarsely.

"It was a crazy plan," Gabe continued. "A stab in the dark, really. After all, the authorities should have made every attempt to find out if you and Joe had any living relatives before the two of you ended up in that children's home. But Ethan still wanted to know. He wanted to be completely certain, for himself and for Joe's sake. And I did too, for you. So we engaged the best agency money could buy. The guys we hired are pros, all former cops and military. If anyone was going to have a chance of unearthing something about your past and Joe's, it was going to be these men and women."

A wave of emotions crashed through Cam as he digested Gabe's words, each stronger than the previous. Fear. Shock. And, most unexpected of all, hope. Such wild hope his knees almost gave out beneath him then.

Gabe's eyes welled up with tears where he stood opposite Cam and his fingers trembled against Cam's skin, as if he too could feel what Cam was experiencing in that moment.

"Cam, this is Sofia Lucciano," Gabe said tremulously. He stepped back, took the hand of the elderly woman watching them, and placed it in Cam's. "She's your grandmother, on your mother's side."

Cam felt his world tilt dizzyingly as he beheld the woman before him.

"Hello, Cameron." Sofia Lucciano squeezed Cam's fingers gently. "Like Gabe said, I'm your grandmother. Your nonna." She sniffed and wiped a tear from her cheek. "Imagine that. Being seventy years old and not knowing I had another grandson in this world." She studied Cameron with a shaky smile. "I can see my Isabella in you. My wild, unpredictable Isabella. You have her eyes." She raised a finger to trace a gentle line down Cam's face. "And that serious expression she always wore." A heavy sigh left her lips then and sadness darkened her features. "I didn't know what happened to her all these years. Not after she vanished that night after she turned sixteen. We looked for her, filed a report with the police and everything. Even hired detectives for a few years. But my Isabella was determined not to be found. I blamed myself for not knowing about the drugs. It was only afterward that I found out she'd fallen in with the wrong crowd at her school. Not that they were even attending school."

Cam swallowed convulsively. His grandmother's eyes were a darker shade of gray than his and the dimples in her wizened face matched the ones in his own cheeks. "So—so my family name is Lucciano?"

Sofia smiled. "It is. But I quite like Sorvino. It was my own grandmother's maiden name after all." Her face crunched up all of a sudden. "Oh darn it to heck! I told them I wouldn't do this but I can't help it! Come here, *mio bellissimo bambino*!" With that, she hauled Cam into her arms, planted a big, fat, wet smooch on his lips, and hugged him so tightly he thought she'd break a rib.

Cam's heart thundered wildly in his chest as he looked over her head at Gabe. "I have a nonna," he said dazedly.

Gabe chuckled and wiped tears from his eyes.

Something his newfound grandmother had just said finally registered on Cam's radar. He pulled back slightly, a corner of his heart already filling with love for the woman in his arms. "Sofia? What did you mean when you said 'them'?"

"Oh." Sofia blinked. "I kinda forgot about them." She sniffed again and rolled her eyes. "Although God knows how, considering how rowdy they all are." She turned and waved an arm toward a row of palm trees some fifty feet away. "You can come out now!" she shouted.

A lightheaded feeling swept over Cam when a horde of twenty or so people suddenly appeared from behind the trees and headed across the beach toward them.

Gabe covered his mouth with one hand, a choked sound bubbling out of him. "Oh my God, the *whole* family came?!" he asked Sofia, his blue eyes dancing with laughter.

Sofia grimaced. "Well, not all of them could make it. And some of them had a stick up their butt about you two being gay and all." She winked at Cam and Gabe. "Stick up their butt? Get it?"

Cam chuckled. "I think that rock over there got it."

Sofia beamed at him. "Anyhow, we'd all been saving up for a family holiday. And we couldn't miss our first gay wedding." She paused and dropped her voice to a whisper, her eyes full of mischief. "Although I suspect we have another gay in the family."

And with that, Cam's new family were upon them.

"Momma, when are we eating?" a little boy with dark hair and gray eyes whined as he pulled on a woman's skirt.

"In a while, my sweet," the woman said, a tremulous smile on her lips as she stared at Cam.

Cam's pulse jumped as he stared back at her. She looked like his mother the way he remembered her on the rare days when she hadn't been high on drugs.

"But I'm *starving!*" the little boy wailed. He

proceeded to stamp his sandaled feet in a way that made Sofia grumble something acerbic under her breath about her family being full of drama queens.

"Emergency sandwich coming up," a man who was evidently the boy's father muttered. He slipped a plastic bag from the rear pocket of his chinos, handed the contents to his son, and watched him gobble it down. "I swear there's a black hole in your stomach, kid."

Two teenage girls dressed in shorts and crop tops giggled behind the man. "*OMG! They are both SO hot!*" one of them hissed to the other. Their eyes were wide with excitement and ill-concealed admiration as they gaped at Cam and Gabe like fangirls who'd just seen their favorite pop stars.

An older boy in a black T-shirt, knee-length shorts, and black kohl eyeliner looked at the girls with a disgusted expression. "You know they're gay, right? As in, they like dick and not pussy?"

The woman standing next to the boy narrowed her eyes and tapped him sharply on the back of the head. "Robert Matteo Lucciano! What did we say about using rude words?"

"Sorry, Mom," the boy mumbled, his cheeks flushing as he glanced at Gabe. "You said we should use the correct terms."

The light that darted in the boy's eyes told Cam he'd just developed a massive crush for Gabe. Cam knew instinctively it was him Sofia had hinted was the other gay in the family.

The boy turned to the girls with a serious expression. "They like penis and not vaginas, 'kay?"

The pot-bellied man beside the boy's mother sighed and rolled his eyes at Cam and Gabe, his resigned expression indicating he'd heard it all before.

"What's a penis?" the little boy with the hunger-induced temper tantrum asked with a wide-eyed expression.

CHAPTER TWENTY-THREE

"What?" Joe whispered, his heart slamming painfully against his ribs. He glanced at the couple and the little girl standing in the shade of a row of trees to the right before staring at Ethan once more.

They were on a deserted stretch of beach close to the resort's pier. To the left, the sun headed steadily toward the horizon, setting the water ablaze with light. The fiery glow washed across Ethan's flushed face and glittering green eyes where he stood opposite Joe, his fingers lightly squeezing Joe's hands. "Her name is Kelly. She is your second cousin on your father's side." Ethan took a shallow breath. "Your parents didn't know they had family when they died in that car crash when you were eight, Joe. Their own parents had cut ties with their relatives a long time back, which is why the authorities couldn't trace anyone who could have taken you in at the time. The private investigators Gabe and I hired didn't manage to find any connections on your mother's side." Ethan smiled tremulously. "But they did on your father's side."

A giddy feeling swept over Joe as the words Ethan had said sunk in. That Ethan and Gabe had hired one of the best detective agencies in the U.S. to look into his and Cam's pasts was shocking enough in its own right. But that the former cops and soldiers had actually come up with a lead not just for one of them, but *both*, was a goddamn miracle.

Ethan worried his lower lip with his teeth, his expression suddenly uncertain. "Are—are you mad at me?"

Joe shook his head slowly, still too stunned to speak.

Relief flooded Ethan's face. He glanced at the couple and the little girl waiting patiently dozens of feet away. "Do you want to meet them?"

Joe swallowed and dipped his chin.

Ethan turned and waved the three figures over.

"Hi, Ethan," the woman said when she stopped in front of them. She kissed Ethan on the cheek and offered her hand to Joe. "I'm Kelly. This is my husband Brian and our daughter Madison."

The man smiled and murmured a greeting to Joe. The little girl hid her face in the folds of her mother's dress with a shy expression that won Joe's heart over in an instant.

Joe took his cousin's hand. "Hi," he managed in a wobbly voice.

Kelly squinted at him, a thin film of tears shimmering in her eyes. "Umm, is it okay if I hug you?"

Heat flooded Joe's face at the emotions her request stirred inside him. He nodded, still not trusting himself to speak. She closed her arms around his waist gingerly.

Joe shuddered and wrapped her in a tight embrace. "I can't believe this is happening," he whispered against her hair, his chest full to bursting. "I can't believe—I can't believe I had someone out there I could have called family all these years!"

"Neither can I," Kelly said, her voice breaking slightly while her tears soaked in Joe's shirt. "I thought I was all alone too, for a long time." She paused and sniffed. "Well, bar our Irish cousins, that is."

Joe stiffened, his pulse stuttering in his veins. He pulled back slightly and stared at Kelly. "What do you mean, Irish cousins?" he mumbled.

Ethan was beaming at him from behind Kelly, his face so full of joy he positively glowed.

Kelly wiped her eyes and smiled up at Joe. "It's not just the two of us. We have a bunch of second and third cousins in Ireland. I found out about them a few years ago." She glanced at her husband. "Brian, Madison, and I visited them for the first time last summer." She grinned at Joe. "I think they're gonna love you."

A babble of voices rose further along the beach.

They turned and beheld a large crowd of men, women, teenagers, and children approaching them. In the midst of them, smiling and laughing, were Gabe and Cam.

Another burst of happiness flooded Joe's heart as he

studied the unfettered joy on his best friend's face. "Is that—"

"Cam's family," Ethan said with a chuckle. "I always knew that bastard had Sicilian blood in him. So, who's ready for food?"

In the end, they moved the wedding rehearsal dinner from a private suite to one of the resort's restaurants to accommodate Gabe's, Cam's, and Joe's families. And long after the wine had flowed and the echoes of laughter as their friends and families got to know one another had died down, Joe and Ethan finally made their way back to their villa under a starlit sky.

Joe slowed when they came abreast of the pier, the idea that had taken shape inside him since even before they arrived at the island now an irrevocable conviction buzzing through his veins. He tugged on Ethan's hand and guided him silently up the wooden steps. They headed all the way to the end of the jetty. Joe pulled Ethan down next to him so they both sat on the edge of the pier with their feet dangling over the water.

He took Ethan's left hand in his own and absent-mindedly stroked his lover's warm skin, his heart and mind still reeling from all that had passed. "So, today's been full of surprises, huh?" he finally murmured.

Ethan grinned at him, faint laughter lines wrinkling the corners of his eyes. "It sure has."

Joe took a deep breath and gathered his nerves for what he was about to do. "I don't want you to think this is because of everything you and Gabe did, or because we're in Hawaii for Cam and Gabe's wedding. This is something I've been thinking about for a while and I think—"

"Yes," Ethan said, his expression suddenly serious as he studied Joe, his green eyes glittering brightly under the starlight.

"What?" Joe mumbled. "But I haven't—"

"I'll marry you."

Joe blinked, stunned all over again. "How did—how did you know I was going to ask you to marry me?!" he stammered.

The sweetest smile curved Ethan's lips. "Because this, right here—," he indicated their surroundings and the dazzling heavens above them, "— is the perfect moment. And if you hadn't asked me first, I would have asked you."

Joe raised shaky fingers to Ethan's face. He traced his beautiful features gently before dropping his forehead against Ethan's. "Do you know how much I love you?" he whispered, his vision blurring.

Ethan shuddered and grasped Joe's hand where it lay against his hot skin. He turned his head and pressed a heated kiss to Joe's palm. "About as much as I love you, I think." Wetness stained Joe's hand from the tears coursing down Ethan's cheeks.

Joe closed his arms around Ethan, his own tears of happiness flowing freely as they held each other in the balmy darkness, the sea singing at their feet while the stars sparkled above them, blessing them in all their brightness.

CHAPTER TWENTY-FOUR

"You nervous?" Ethan said.

Gabe took a shallow breath and shook his head. "I don't think so."

"Really? 'Cause I would be shitting bricks if I was in your shoes right now," Ethan said bluntly.

Gabe chuckled as Ethan pinned the dark gray rose to the lapel of his cream Gucci tuxedo. Ethan stepped back and scanned him critically from the top of his carefully arranged, slicked-back hair, to his gleaming black dress shoes.

"Looking mighty fine, Mr. Anderson," Ethan drawled, his eyes sparkling with appreciation.

Gabe stared at his reflection in the floor-length mirror of his and Cam's bedroom. "You think so?" he said, worrying his lower lip with his teeth as a sudden bout of apprehension flashed through him.

Ethan chuckled. "I *know* so. Cam's gonna have a heart attack when he sees you."

A knock came on the glass sliding door overlooking

the villa's deck. Gabe's father stepped inside the room. He stopped and rocked back on his heels when he saw Gabe.

Gabe swallowed convulsively at the flash of raw emotion in his father's eyes.

George Anderson recovered his composure and cleared his throat. "Are you ready, son?"

Gabe nodded shakily and dug his nails into his palms to stem the tears threatening to overwhelm him. "Yes, Dad."

With Ethan leading the way, Gabe's father walked Gabe over to the garden where his and Cam's wedding was to take place.

❧

CAM TENSED SLIGHTLY AS THE STRING QUARTET STRUCK up the music for "The Only Exception" by Paramore. He turned where he stood waiting under the flower-wreathed wedding arch on the wooden stage overlooking the beach and the crystal-clear lagoon, Joe and the female minister officiating his and Gabe's wedding at his side.

The setting sun cast golden fingers over the stunningly decorated grounds and the guests sitting in the rows of chairs packing the lawn opposite him. They'd had to add additional seats for the extra guests who'd turned up for the wedding, and Cam's newfound family beamed at him where they crowded the rows to the right of the stage, the women already sniffing and dabbing at their eyes. Even Eveline and Lana were struggling to mask their tears behind their dazzling smiles where they sat with the rest of their friends in the front rows.

Then Gabe appeared and the world faded around Cam. His heart thumped rapidly against his ribs as his eyes locked with the cobalt-blue ones of the drop-dead gorgeous man in the cream tuxedo walking slowly down the flower-strewn aisle toward him. A dark gray rose the exact shade of Cam's eyes sat in a spray of small red flowers on Gabe's left lapel.

Then Gabe was on the stage next to him. And Gabe's father was murmuring words and handing Gabe's hand over to Cam while Ethan took up his position as Gabe's best man.

And Cam found himself standing in front of the man he loved and had to stop himself from pinching his own hand. Because he couldn't believe someone like Gabe was his. Had been his since that night they first met, so many moons ago. And had promised to be his for the rest of both their lives.

❦

NOTHING EXISTED OUTSIDE OF THIS MOMENT. NOT their remarkable surroundings. Not their happy, crying guests. Not even the minister who stood smiling at them in her smart white dress suit.

Gabe couldn't look away from Cam where he stood opposite him in a stunning pale gray tuxedo. A wobbly smile curved Gabe's lips as he glanced at the blue rose decorating Cam's lapel. It matched the color of Gabe's eyes. He looked up and met Cam's gaze once more.

Cam smiled faintly and leaned in toward Gabe. "We had the same idea," he whispered, looking at the gray flower on Gabe's tuxedo.

"So we did," Gabe replied with a low chuckle.

"Hey, it's *way* too early for kissing, you two!" Ethan said in a loud stage whisper that had their guests chuckling and Joe sighing.

And then the minister started speaking. "On behalf of Cameron and Gabe, I would like to thank you and welcome you on this beautiful day to celebrate their wedding."

As the words of the ceremony washed over them, Gabe kept his eyes locked on Cam and Cam on his, their fingers clasped tightly together, their rings gleaming in the light of the setting sun.

Then it was time for their vows.

"Cam and Gabe, I believe you have some words to share with one another and your guests," the minister said.

Gabe swallowed. Cam squeezed his hands, his gray eyes bright with encouragement.

"All my adult life, I have searched for someone who could make me feel whole," Gabe started slowly. "Someone who could be my partner in all my challenges and my successes. To enjoy the happy times and bear the sad times with. Someone to share my years with as I grow old." He bit his lower lip. Cam let go of Gabe's left hand and touched his thumb gently to Gabe's mouth, wordlessly halting the nervous movement, a faint smile curving his own lips. Gabe let out a shuddering breath as Cam lowered his hand to take his once more. "At first, I thought that person was meant to be a woman. So I tried for some time, despite the fact that it felt wrong deep down inside. And then I realized I was gay. And I started searching for a man instead. That one man I could belong to and who would belong to me." He faltered for a moment. "I didn't find him. Not at first. And I went through some dark times. Times that I thought would never end." Gabe paused and gazed into Cam's glittering eyes, knowing he too was remembering their first night together and Gabe's heart-rending confession. "And then I walked into the last place I ever imagined I would find that man. And there he was." His voice grew stronger. 'There *you* were, Cam. And every day with you since then has filled my life with more happiness than I ever imagined possible. We've laughed. We've cried. We've fought. We've made love." Gabe grinned. "And *boy*, have we made love."

"Like bunnies," Ethan whispered to their guests.

Laughter broke out among the crowd.

"You were my first man, Cam," Gabe said. "And I would be honored if you would be my last, for as long as I live."

SILENCE DESCENDED AROUND THEM AS GABE COMPLETED his vows while the sun finally sank below the horizon. Cam's pulse raced as he stared at Gabe, his heart full to bursting at the emotions he could feel vibrating off Gabe in strong, warm waves. The emotions he could see in his eyes and feel in his touch. He inhaled deeply as Gabe squeezed his hands and encouraged him in return.

"My childhood was not a happy one and it made me a bitter man," Cam began in a low voice. "A man who shunned love not because he didn't believe in it, but because he didn't think he would ever be able to reciprocate the feeling."

A low sob reached his ears from the row of guests. Cam paused and gazed across to his grandmother. He flashed her a tremulous smile when he saw the tears streaming down her face.

"It's okay," he said quietly.

She nodded and wiped her eyes.

Cam looked at Gabe and arched an eyebrow. "Italians, huh?"

Chuckles rose from the crowd. The minister beamed.

Cam's fingers tightened around Gabe's. "I didn't know that night when you walked into *Saron* that you'd also walked into my heart. I didn't know then why I felt so much for you from the get go. Why I wanted to protect and cherish you as much as I wanted to rip the clothes off your body and, well—," he directed the most wicked smile at Gabe while Gabe blushed a bright pink, "—you know."

"The whole world and their dogs know, Cam!" Eveline called out from the front row while their guests broke out in peals of laughter.

"Amen to that," Ethan stated with a grin.

Cam sobered as he stared at Gabe. "That night you confessed to me was both the best and worst night of my life. Best because there you were, the most beautiful, precious human being I had ever had the privilege to be with, declaring his love for me. Worst because there I was, a man convinced he was a broken shell incapable of returning that incredible love."

Tears pooled in Gabe's eyes and flowed down his flushed cheeks in the soft glow of the giant candle-lit lanterns and flame torches lighting up the fairy-tale-like setting of their wedding.

Cam gently wiped the wet trails on Gabe's cheeks before raising Gabe's left hand to his mouth and pressing a kiss to his knuckles, his chest constricting with emotion.

"It took me a while to get there," Cam continued. "To the place where you were waiting for me, with your big, wonderful, generous heart full of so much love it still blinds me to this day. So, let me repeat to you the words I said two months ago." Cam cradled Gabe's face in his hands and pressed his forehead against Gabe's, the shivers coursing through Gabe's body dancing down his own spine. "Gabe, you've taught me so much in the two years we've been together. You've taught me to be bold and to dare take a chance on you. On us. On this crazy, wonderful love. You've taught me to laugh. You've taught me how to fight and make up, rather spectacularly I might add." He smiled when laughter broke out around them once more. "Every day I spend with you is another day I thank the heavens for the gift they granted me when they gave me you. So, please take my hand, Gabe. And lead me on this path we have both chosen. This bright path full of light and the myriad colors of our love. I, for one, cannot wait to see what else you will teach me as we build our family and grow old together."

Silence wrapped around the two of them as Cam completed his vows. Then the crowd jumped to their feet and erupted in loud cheers and claps.

"You guys," Ethan sniffed, wiping tears from his face. Joe passed him a handkerchief, his own eyes gleaming with wetness.

And so the minister blessed their union and uttered the final words of the ceremony.

"Cameron Anderson-Sorvino and Gabe Anderson-Sorvino, I now declare you husband and husband. You may kiss your groom."

And the crowd went wild again as Cam swept Gabe into his arms, bent him backward at the waist, and swooped down to take his lips in a blistering kiss full of promise.

As the string quartet broke out in "Signed, Sealed, Delivered, I'm Yours," Cam and Gabe stepped down the stage into the arms of their friends and their families old and new.

Soon, the gardens were rearranged with tables and chairs for the wedding dinner, and a wooden deck was put together in the middle of the lawn for the dance party. As the night wore on and the stars came out in their millions, Ethan and Joe regaled their guests with embarrassing tales from Cam and Gabe's relationship and Cam's time in the children's home he'd shared with Joe, including the one about the prostitutes and Cam's first kiss. Then it was time for Cam and Gabe's first dance as a couple.

They stepped onto the stage to the hypnotic lyrics and tunes of "Everything" by Alanis Morissette, their friends and families watching on with wide smiles on their faces. And as they swayed and twisted and turned to the music, Cam kissed Gabe and whispered, "Thank you."

Gabe tilted his head to the side, his blue eyes puzzled.

"For saying yes," Cam breathed against his lips. "Not just to marrying me. Thank you for saying yes that night when we first met."

Gabe smiled and kissed him back.

CHAPTER TWENTY-FIVE

Gabe opened the door to their apartment and headed inside ahead of Cam. He eyed the pile of mail Ethan had placed on the console table in the hallway during their absence and dropped their hand luggage on the floor. Cam rolled their cases in behind him and closed the door.

Gabe turned to him. "We're home," he said with a bittersweet sigh.

Cam smiled, his teeth white against his tanned skin. "That we are."

It was Saturday morning and they'd just returned from their honeymoon. Although Gabe missed Hawaii and the heavenly time they'd spent at Lincoln's resort, he was also pleased to be back in Tokyo.

"So, Mr. Anderson-Sorvino," Gabe said in a teasing tone as he strolled up to Cam and looped his arms around Cam's waist. "What should we do on the first day of the rest of our lives?"

Cam closed his arms around Gabe and dropped a

kiss on his head. "Why, Mr. Anderson-Sorvino, I think the answer should be obvious." He lowered his hands and fondled Gabe's butt.

Gabe pulled back slightly and narrowed his eyes at his husband. "If I didn't know any better, I'd say you were with me just for my body."

Cam grinned and pressed his lips to Gabe's. "I kinda like your mind, too."

Gabe let out a dreamy breath and lost himself in Cam's intoxicating kiss. A moan of protest escaped him when Cam reluctantly wrenched his lips free a moment later.

"Actually, there's something I want to do," Cam said. "Later."

They had a light breakfast, showered, and napped for a couple of hours before getting up and unpacking. It was early afternoon by the time Cam grabbed the keys to the Jag and dragged Gabe out of the apartment. Despite Gabe's questioning, Cam refused to tell him where they were going and only smiled at him enigmatically. As the car ate away the miles to their mysterious destination, Gabe dozed off to the soft sounds of jazz music playing from the car's speakers. He woke up with a jolt some time later and saw that they'd stopped on a deserted gravel driveway.

Dusk was falling across the land. Ahead and to the left of the track, a grassy embankment fell away to a small pebbly beach and the clear blue-green waters of a shallow cove. A green hill rose to the right of the driveway. Built into the side of the verdant slope was a pretty, one-story, traditional Japanese house with a red-tiled pitched roof and broad eaves. A beautiful Japanese garden stood to the side of the property and merged with the woodland rising behind it. There was no one about and no other properties that he could see.

Gabe realized Cam was sitting in the driver's seat watching him with an expectant expression. He gave his husband a puzzled look. "Where are we?"

Cam didn't reply. Instead, he smiled faintly, stepped out of the car, and took Gabe's hand when he joined him on the track. Cam led him silently up the quaint, winding stone path rising to the house under the reddening sky.

Gabe's eyes widened when Cam took a key from his pocket and opened the front door. "Cam?" he murmured, mystified.

Cam flicked lights on as he walked through the property. Gabe followed, his hand still firmly clasped in Cam's, his bewildered gaze sweeping the empty house.

Cam finally stopped in a room with dual-aspect views over the garden and the beach and let go of Gabe's hand. Gabe stared from the low, made-up king-size bed dominating the tatami floor and the overnight bag sitting atop the sheets, to the soft lanterns Cam was lighting as he walked around the chamber.

The soft trickle of water from the pond in the garden reached Gabe's ears as Cam slid the windows open. Gabe crossed the room slowly and picked up the note on the bed next to the overnight bag.

It was from Ethan and read, *"There's food in the pantry. See you soon!"*

Gabe looked up to find Cam gazing at him. "What's going on, Cam?"

Cam smiled at him and beckoned him over to the window. Gabe joined him, still at a loss as to what was going on.

Cam positioned Gabe in front of the opening and wrapped his arms around his waist from behind. "Look over there," he murmured, pointing straight ahead.

Gabe followed Cam's gaze out over the beach and the cove to the ocean beyond. Lights sparkled on a distant shore across a narrow bay.

Gabe drew a sharp breath when he finally realized where they were. "This is the Izu Peninsula," he breathed.

"Yes," Cam said.

Gabe's heart started a steady drumming against his ribs as he stared at the bright constellation directly opposite the house, on the other side of the expanse of darkening water.

"Is that—"

"The inn you took me to last year?" Cam said quietly. "The one where you told me you loved me? Yes, it is."

Gabe twisted in Cam's arms and stared at him.

Cam rubbed his nose against Gabe's and smiled. "This is my wedding gift to you."

Gabe blinked. "What is?"

Cam looked around the bedroom. "This house."

"What?!" Gabe gasped.

Cam grinned at his shocked expression. "I saw this place after we came back from the States. I wasn't sure whether to buy it at first, but Joe and Ethan convinced me it was perfect for us. Ethan even negotiated a deal with the realtor and picked up the keys while we were in Hawaii. He left them for us in the glove compartment of the car."

"But—but why?!" Gabe spluttered.

"Because although I love our place in Tokyo, I thought this would make a perfect getaway for when we want some time away from the city. There are enough rooms for guests if our friends want to visit." Cam paused and dropped a light kiss on Gabe's lips. "And because this is where you first told me you loved me."

Emotion clogged Gabe's throat as he gazed into Cam's eyes. "God, you're such a hopeless romantic," he said in a choked voice.

"Does that mean you like it?" Cam asked, a note of uncertainty underscoring his voice.

Gabe looped his arms around Cam's neck. "I love it. Thank you. This is more than I deserve."

Cam beamed and took Gabe's mouth in a long, slow kiss.

All too soon, the passion between them ignited and they undressed each other hastily under a rising moon. And as the night wore on, they made love, at times passionately and at times slowly, their cries and moans echoing around the empty rooms of their new home and across the garden to the beach down the hill.

CHAPTER TWENTY-SIX

ETHAN STARED AT ASH. "IS THAT AN ENGAGEMENT RING on your finger?!"

Everyone's gaze dropped from Ash's flushed cheeks to the elegant metal band on his left hand as he climbed on the bar stool.

"Luke asked me to marry him," the Colby heir admitted shyly, glancing at the man standing beside him.

It was the week before Christmas and everyone had gathered at *Saron* for an early celebration, Ash and Luke flying in from Singapore and Lana and Tom joining them from Shanghai for the weekend. It was the first time all of them were together since Cam and Gabe's wedding.

Luke smiled and wrapped an arm around Ash's waist. "It was well overdue," he murmured, ruffling Ash's hair with his lips. "Besides, the number of women throwing themselves at this kid's feet since he started working was seriously beginning to piss me off."

"Ah-ha," Eveline said with a grin. "So, you're just marking your territory?"

"I get the feeling Luke marks his territory in plenty other ways," Wade drawled, his gaze on the fresh hickey on Ash's neck.

Ash blushed fiercely, much to everyone's amusement.

"So, how's wedded life suiting you two?" Lana asked Gabe and Cam.

They exchanged smiles. "It's good," Gabe said quietly.

"It's more than good," Cam murmured, dropping a kiss on his husband's lips. "It's goddamn perfect."

"If it wasn't for the fact that I am also a soon-to-be-married man, I would be seriously disgusted right now," Ethan said tartly.

"This wedding bug really is catching," Rhys said with a grin, linking his hand with Wade's. An engagement ring gleamed on their fingers.

"So, anyone got a date in mind yet?" Lincoln asked. "Eveline and I were thinking next year."

"Oh?" Tom raised an eyebrow. "Lana and I are thinking next year too, after the baby is born."

"So are we," Ethan said.

"Same here," Luke murmured.

"Ditto," Wade said.

Gabe straightened on his bar stool and studied his friends with an intense expression, a crazy idea taking shape in his mind. "November," he stated.

They all stared at him.

"On our anniversary," Gabe continued, excitement

surging through him as he glanced at Cam. "Why don't you all get married in one year? We'll all share the same wedding day and—"

"We'll be able to celebrate our anniversaries on the same day every year," Ethan said, his green eyes sparkling with delight. "It'd be another reason for us to get together."

"That's a crazy idea," Eveline said, her blue eyes wide.

"Crazy good or crazy bad?" Lincoln asked pensively. "'Cause I kinda like it."

"Crazy good!" Lana and Eveline exclaimed at the same time.

They laughed and exchanged thrilled glances.

"I like it too," Luke said. He took Ash's hand and kissed his knuckles, his amber eyes glowing warmly.

"I second that," Ash said.

"That's a yes for us, too," Rhys said. Wade nodded.

"Tom?" Lana asked.

"Sounds good to me," Tom said with a smile.

Ethan looked at Joe. "What do you think?"

Joe wrapped his arms around Ethan and kissed his cheek. "I think it's a wonderful idea. I've got one question though. Where the hell are we going to do this?"

"Well, we can use my resort again," Lincoln suggested.

"Or our island," Ash said. He glanced at Luke. "Our place should be ready by then." Luke dipped his chin.

Ethan arched an eyebrow and looked around their group. "So, we're really setting the date?"

Everyone grinned.

"We're setting the date," Rhys said.

They raised their glasses and toasted one another.

THE END

Don't miss the Nights Series Short Story Collection! Catch up with your favorite couples from the series in this exclusive collection. Get it today in my author store.

Discover a brand new hot and sexy small town romance series about a group of best friends! Meet Alex, Carter, Hunter, Wyatt, Drake, Tristan, and Miles. They will make you laugh. They will make you cry. They *will* wreck you. And they will make you fall in love with them just as hard as they do.

Get Alex (Twilight Falls #1) Turn the page to read an extract now!

ALEX (TWILIGHT FALLS #1)
SPECIAL PREVIEW

ALEX HANCOCK CAME OUT OF THE COFFEE SHOP opposite the courthouse and froze in his tracks.

Someone had parked their dirty, mud-streaked Jeep Wrangler close to his pristine, black and red Triumph motorcycle.

Alex's knuckles whitened on his cup of black coffee.

When it rains, it fucking pours!

He stormed across the street, stopped in front of the offending vehicle, and glared at it as if it had committed a crime. A car slowly pulled up behind him.

"Wow," someone murmured. "You look pissed."

Alex turned. A pretty brunette was watching him with an amused expression from behind the wheel of a red, convertible Mini.

"You would be too if some asshole just blocked you in!" he snapped.

Izzy Batista's green eyes sparkled impishly as she observed the grimy, four-wheel drive. "Yup, that guy must be one giant dick."

She parked her car and joined him outside the courthouse.

"I gotta give it to you, Hancock. You sure scrub up nice." Izzy placed her hands on her hips and scrutinized him with a critical eye.

Alex sighed irritably and downed his drink. He winced when a burst of acid rose in his throat.

"Easy on the coffee, stud," Izzy murmured. "We don't want you getting an ulcer on your big day."

A fresh bout of nerves twisted Alex's gut at Izzy's words.

"I can't believe I'm doing this," he mumbled to himself. "Me, Alex Hancock, getting married."

Izzy patted his arm. "No backsies." A trace of steel underscored her friendly tone. "Remember, you got a lot riding on this."

He crushed the coffee cup and tossed it in a nearby trash can.

She's right.

It had been a month since the life Alex had carefully built in San Diego had come crashing down around him, after his business partner of two years embezzled from their law firm and ran off to Mexico. Mired in debt and with his new condo on the verge of being repossessed, Alex had desperately been trying to raise the necessary capital to salvage his career and company when Izzy Batista had called him out of the blue ten days ago. The sister of Wyatt Batista, one of Alex's lifelong friends from his hometown of Twilight Falls, Izzy had discovered the predicament he was in through her older brother.

"I may have a solution to your problems," Izzy said. *"Word of warning though, it's pretty unorthodox."*

Alex stilled where he sat on his couch, his cell phone in hand. "What do you mean?"

"One of my clients is in trouble," Izzy said. *"They have to get married by the end of the month or they'll lose their estate and half of their considerable fortune."*

Alex frowned. "I don't understand."

Izzy sighed. "I'm saying this client needs a mail-order groom. And pronto. They're willing to pay half a million dollars to the right candidate."

Alex's mouth went dry. "Half a million dollars?" His heart pounded against his ribs as he glanced at the boxes filling the apartment. He'd barely started unpacking when Ryan had pulled the rug out from under him and disappeared with half the company's funds.

"Yup, half a million dollars," Izzy repeated. *"The contract's for six months. Marry the client, live with them, and then walk into the sunset with the money and no strings attached."*

Alex swallowed, shocked that he was even entertaining the crazy idea Izzy had just proposed.

"Where does your client live?" he mumbled.

"Twilight Falls."

Alex grimaced at Izzy's answer. He raked a hand through his hair and stared at the dazzling lights of San Diego Bay through the glass doors overlooking his terrace, a storm of memories and bittersweet emotions crashing over him.

"I know you don't like coming back here, Alex," Izzy said quietly. *"Not since the accident. But this could solve all your problems. And my client's too."*

Alex chewed the inside of his cheek. "What's wrong with your client?"

"What makes you think there's anything wrong with my client?" Izzy said in a voice that Alex immediately distrusted.

"Because someone with that much money shouldn't be struggling to find herself a fiancé, even a fake one. So what is it? Is she unattractive? Does she have a horrible personality?" He pulled a face. "Does she eat puppies for breakfast?"

"None of the above," Izzy replied in a cheerful tone. "The client is gorgeous. They're just a bit...eccentric, is all."

Alex mulled Izzy's words over. Eccentric he could deal with.

"Are they expecting sex?"

A soft chuckle travelled down the line.

"No, it isn't that kind of arrangement. Besides, I know you're more into dicks than vaginas."

"Yeah, well, my dick hasn't seen much action lately," Alex muttered.

"And here I thought you moved to San Diego for all the gay guys," Izzy said drily. "You know, since you'd pretty much fucked all the hot ones here in Twilight Falls."

Alex scowled. "I only fucked one hot guy in that town."

Izzy laughed. Alex found his lips curving in a faint smile at her bubbly voice. Truth be told, he missed Izzy and Wyatt. He missed all the friends he'd left behind when he decided to move to San Diego, after the accident that had changed all of their lives.

A comfortable silence settled between them.

"So, what will it be, Alex?" Izzy finally said.

Alex hesitated. "The end of the month is only ten days away."

"Your math is spot on. I knew there was a reason why you became a lawyer."

Alex ignored her sarcastic words. "Give me a few days to think about it."

It had taken him three days to make his decision. Six days later, he'd put his stuff in storage, returned his apartment keys to his realtor, and climbed on the beautifully restored, classic motorcycle he'd owned since he was seventeen for the one-hundred-and-fifty-mile ride to the San Bernardino Mountains and the quaint, historic town of Twilight Falls.

Nestled in a valley of towering pine forests and home to the picturesque waterfall and rapids from which it took its name, Twilight Falls started life as a nineteenth-century trading post and mining settlement, during the California Gold Rush. After a slump following the two World Wars, the place saw a strong revival in the second half of the twentieth century, as a result of a sustained campaign by the city council to turn it into a tourist town. The rise in outdoor sports activities meant it now stayed busy pretty much all year around, with the briefest of lulls at Thanksgiving and the New Year.

Alex had reached Twilight Falls late last night. Having refused Izzy and Wyatt's offer to put him up at their place, he'd booked himself into a motel outside town; the spring tourist season was just getting started and there'd still been rooms available at short notice. Not that he would have wanted to stay in town. Even though it had been twelve years since he'd left the place, he was bound to bump into someone he knew and he wasn't in the mood for small talk.

"Are you ready?" Izzie said presently, excitement raising the pitch of her voice.

"Not really," Alex murmured.

Izzy grinned. "Yeah, well, if you'd stayed at our place, we could have gotten you wasted and you'd be doing this drunk right now."

"I really don't think the county clerk would be impressed if the groom turned up with a hangover," Alex said sternly. "Besides, I'm entering a legal agreement with this woman. The least I can do is show up sober."

He looked up at the two-story, cream stucco and red-brick building before them and squared his shoulders.

Whoever this broad is, I only have to live with her for six months. How bad can it be?

An odd expression danced across Izzy's face.

"What is it?" Alex said.

"Nothing." Izzy flashed him a bright smile, hooked her arm through his elbow, and guided him up the short flight of steps and into the building.

They checked in at reception and headed in the direction of the court rooms. Surprise darted through Alex when Izzy walked past the austere wooden doors and continued down the hall.

"Where are we going?" he said, puzzled.

"To the chapel," Izzy replied breezily.

He arched an eyebrow.

"The client insisted," she explained with a mysterious smile.

The first tendrils of unease started coiling through Alex. Izzy was acting strange. And he wasn't sure he liked the hint of devilment in the depths of her eyes.

The chapel doors appeared up ahead. Alex's pulse speeded up when they opened them and stepped inside a large, airy chamber. The chapel was a relatively new addition to the courthouse and had been designed along the traditional lines of a church, with an altar, a chancel, and a nave split by a central aisle. But it wasn't the charming ecclesiastical interior or the delightful pastel colors around them that caused Alex to draw a sharp breath and rock to a stop on the checkered marble flooring.

He stared beyond the bright posies and white lace decorating the wooden pews to the two figures rising to their feet from the front right row.

"Jesus, Izzy!" Alex hissed, shock reverberating through him. "I can't marry her! She's older than my grandmother!"

The elderly dame in the pink brocade dress and pale floral hat arched an eyebrow.

"You were right," she told Izzy. "That one has a smart mouth on him." The woman's eyes fairly twinkled with glee as she studied Alex's stunned expression. "I'm not the one you're marrying, sonny."

Alex's heart stuttered. His gaze switched to the tall, dark-haired man in the smart, navy-blue suit and the ivory, rose boutonnière next to the woman. A thunderous expression clouded the stranger's handsome, stubbled features.

Shit. You're kidding me.

"What the hell is going on, Izzy?" the man growled.

Read Alex today

AFTERWORD

To all my friends who helped make this possible. You know who you are.

To you, my readers. Thank you for reading One Day! I cannot begin to tell you how much fun I had writing this series finale. I hope you enjoyed seeing your favorite characters and experiencing all their Happy Ever Afters once more. I would be grateful if you could leave a review on Goodreads or on the store where you purchased this book. Reviews help readers like you find my books and I truly appreciate your honest opinions about my stories.

Make sure to sign up to my store newsletter for special deals on my books and new release alerts. Or you can sign up to my author newsletter instead to get upcoming release notifications, sneak peeks, and giveaways.

Ava Marie Salinger is the romance pen name of an Amazon bestselling author with a passion for writing addictive tales. Known for her action-packed and thrilling urban fantasy novels, she has expanded her repertoire with the introduction of the M/M urban fantasy romance series Fallen Messengers. Additionally, she has penned the scorching hot contemporary M/M romance series Nights and Twilight Falls as A.M. Salinger. When not immersed in her writing, Ava can be found curating inspiring music playlists, indulging in her love for nature, marveling at the latest gadgets, and savoring Chinese cuisine.

You can find all of Ava's books on her author store at shop.adstarrling.com